Beg For Mercy

Detective Solomon Gray, Volume 3

Keith Nixon

Published by Gladius Press, 2019.

Beg For Mercy
A Solomon Gray Novel
Keith Nixon

Prologue

Fifteen Years Ago

Valerie Usher rolled off to lie by his side. Beads of sweat dripped from her body, along with her anger and frustration.

He put out a hand to take Valerie's, to apologise, but she flinched and pushed him away. Valerie pulled the bed sheet over herself then shielded her eyes with a forearm to distance herself from him. The heat rose in his face, and he bunched the sheet up in his grip until the moment passed.

Staring at the ceiling, he wondered yet again why he was here. But he already knew the answer. *Lust.* From the moment he'd first spied her in that form-fitting evening dress, hugging every one of her luscious curves, he knew he had to have her. She was his forbidden fruit. Before, he'd felt drawn to Valerie like a piece of metal to a magnet, unable to resist. Afterwards the guilt kicked in.

"Are you thinking about your wife again?" asked Valerie. "Is that why you couldn't get it up?"

The mattress bounced as Valerie shifted her weight to face him. He turned his head. Valerie was on her side now, an arm crooked, her head resting on a hand. He smelt the hint of cooled sweat. Instead of answering, he ran his eyes down the shape of her body shrouded beneath the sheet. Valerie placed her palm on his chest and felt his heartbeat accelerate. "I want you to leave her," she said.

"We've been through this," he sighed. "I can't."

"Why?"

"We're married."

"But you're screwing me."

"So?"

Valerie rolled onto him, straddling him, allowing the sheet to fall away. She leaned down so her eyes were inches away from his. He felt her breath, hot on his face, smelt a hint of coffee.

"Unless you tell her, this is the last time you'll have me." Valerie flexed her hips, making him groan. He closed his eyes, enjoying the moment. "We can make this work. Leave her, move into your own place." He felt her lips on his chest, then his stomach, his hips, his cock.

"No," he said, pushing her off.

A flash of anger crossed Valerie's features, as if she'd never been denied before. *No*. A word she didn't quite understand.

"I've told you," she said, "we're done if you won't."

"Then we're done," he sighed, even though he hoped it wasn't so.

Valerie laughed briefly, the stopped when she caught the look on his face. She leaned backwards, groped at his groin.

He pushed her hand away. "We shouldn't be doing this. Get off me."

Her hand went to his chest, lacing her fingers through his chest hair once more. "What would your friends think about you having an affair?"

They'd be shocked. The churchgoing man with a young family and respectable job. He taught his son's Sunday school class, for Christ's sakes.

Valerie took a handful of his hair and pulled. He grimaced. "Then I'll tell your boss." Another tug. "The cop shagging the snitch." She yanked the hair this time, harder, painful. "You'll be divorced, friendless, and out of a job." She wrenched at him again and snarled. "Your reputation ruined. I'll hollow you out."

"Stop."

"So, you'll leave her?" She sat back and lifted her eyebrows in amusement.

"I can't." Even to him, his voice sounded wheedling, weak.

In a sudden swipe, she slapped him. His cheek stung. As she raised her hand to hit him on the other side of his face, he caught her arm mid-swing. Valerie lunged forward, biting into his arm. He shouted in pain, lashing out with a fist. It caught her on the cheekbone, and she rolled off him.

"You bastard!" Valerie's hand darted up to where he'd hit her. With her other hand, she gathered the sheet up around herself. She glared at him with such intensity, he should have burst into flames.

"You're pathetic," she spat, rubbing her cheek. "You can't even get it up. No wonder your own wife won't fuck you anymore."

"Shut up."

"It's over. And so is your perfect little life. I'm telling Duncan everything."

"I said, shut up!"

"I'll make him kill you slowly. You pathetic excuse for a man."

He pounced on her, wrapping his fingers around her throat, just to shut her up. He couldn't stand it anymore. The taunts. The threats. The jibes. Valerie clawed at his arms forcing his head upwards, but he exerted more pressure. She tried to shove him back, her hand at his chin. She bucked and kicked, trying to put a knee into his balls. He was too heavy, too strong for her. As the seconds crawled, Valerie weakened. She tried to push him off again, but the drag of her fingernails felt more like a caress. Her hand dropped away and landed on the mattress with a thud. Valerie gave one last lurch before she died.

The real world rushed back to him. *Shit.* He looked at his fingers, then at Valerie, her jaw so wide open he could see a dark filling in her back tooth. *Had he really killed her?* He placed two fingers on the side of her neck, feeling for a pulse. He hoped it had been a dream, but he knew she was gone. He hoped her soul was at rest, because his would never be again. He got off the bed, pulled out his mobile phone, and made a call. *Confession time.*

While he waited he pulled the pillow off the floor and put it over her face. He couldn't stomach the accusatory look.

One

Always be ready, because you never know what you're going to find.

That's what Detective Constable Solomon Gray and his classmates were told by the instructor at the Maidstone police training college.

Being the first responder at a potential crime scene meant certain responsibilities. Others were on their way, Gray just happened to be the nearest Crime Investigation Department Officer. He had to admit, he was excited at the idea. *This was it.* He hoped it was a big one.

Gray swung his car onto Castle Avenue and found his way blocked by a squad car. The revolving lights cast a steel blue hue across Castle Avenue, part of the quiet residential area known in Broadstairs as the Chessboard because all the roads were named after the game's pieces. Pleasant detached residences on Castle Avenue, a low to non-existent crime rate, home to the better-heeled on the Isle of Thanet.

Gray killed the engine and stepped into the warm night – an unexpected heatwave in early October – some shift in the jet stream bringing unseasonable weather to the south east. After the relative cool of the car's air-conditioned interior, the out-side temperature was thick and sticky. This time of year, the air should have been crisp to accompany the falling leaves.

Gusts of wind from the nearby cliffs carried a brief respite of cool and the swish of beating waves. The sea was just a five-minute walk away. Otherwise, silence. Gray leaned into the un-manned squad car and switched the blues off. For a moment everything appeared normal. No outward sign of disturbance – a single bystander, a man on the pavement with a dog – oth-erwise just a couple of curtain-twitchers peering out at the un-usual commotion. It was late, nearing 11 p.m. The residents here were too polite to impose. Until Constable Mike Fowler motioned Gray over and said, "He's over here, Sol."

Fowler, a beat cop, was a bulky man, muscle filling out his uniform. A short-sleeved white shirt revealed firm arms. He shaved his hair right to the scalp and wore a permanent frown beneath the brim of his cap, pulled down low. He was a poster boy of an imposing cop, portraying the don't-mess-with-me persona. Invaluable on a Saturday night when the Margate pubs kicked out.

"Is the perimeter secure?" asked Gray.

"Of course. I know my job." Fowler and Gray had joined the force at the same time, but Gray had reached CID first. Fowler was still sulking, but Gray hadn't the time for petty sen-timents; only one thing on his mind.

"What did you find?"

"Don't you know?"

"I'd like to hear it from you."

"The body of a woman, upstairs. No immediate signs of cause of death. Don't worry, I didn't trample the crime scene, I entered under the purpose of preservation of life. I checked her pulse. Didn't even turn the lights on. Then I left, waited for the cavalry to turn up. But got you." Fowler shrugged, like he shouldn't have been expecting much.

"Where's the guy who called it in?"

"Over there." Fowler hiked a thumb over his shoulder.

"Take me to him."

Fowler, fists clenched and shoulders hunched, led Gray to the man standing on the pavement, under the sodium yellow hue of a street light. The man wore shorts, flip-flops and a t-shirt. A chocolate labrador lay at his feet, unmoved by the proceedings of humans, uninterested in Gray.

"I'll leave you to it," said Fowler and walked away without awaiting a reply.

"Are you Mr Lavater?" asked Gray.

"Yes." Lavater's white hair was thinning and scraped across to cover a bald patch. He patted at it subconsciously, expertly pushing a few strands back into place.

"Beautiful dog." Gray knelt and scratched behind the labrador's ear, eliciting a tail wag in response. Gray got back to his feet. "Tell me what happened."

"I was walking past, with Cadbury, and I noticed the gate was wide open." Lavater pointed. Gray turned to follow Lavater's indication but couldn't see any detail from where he was standing. The house sat recessed from the road. Lavater's accent wasn't local. Sounded like one of the many Londoners who'd bought a property out of the city and commuted, accepting a long daily commute, the early starts and the late finishes in exchange for the seaside air.

"When I came back half an hour later, it was the same," said Lavater. "I was surprised and concerned, normally the gates are closed. Mrs Usher keeps to herself, so I went to see if there was something wrong."

"Usher?" interrupted Gray. "Any relation to Duncan Usher?"

"I've no idea. Sorry."

Maybe she was married to the local crime boss, Duncan Usher? If so, this was going to be a huge deal. Gray wrote a few words in his notebook, his hand shaking. Gray paused briefly at the arrival of another squad car, disgorging two uniforms. They ignored Gray, heading straight for Fowler. Operating along tribal lines.

"You entered the property, sir?"

"Not precisely. I stopped at the front door, shouted inside but nobody replied. So I called you lot. Crime scene contamination and all that." Lavater even winked.

An armchair CSI, thought Gray. He managed to restrain the sigh.

"Has anyone taken a statement from you?"

"Not yet."

"Then I'll need you to stay here until one of my colleagues does so."

Lavater frowned. "I've got a 6 a.m. train to catch in the morning."

A white van – "Forensics" stamped on the side – rolled along the road.

"Thank you for your cooperation, sir."

Gray turned away before Lavater could protest further. Fowler would have to deal with him. Gray headed for the van, arriving as the Crime Scene Manager, Sean Brazier, unfolded from the passenger side. Brazier was tall and thin – ungainly like a human stick insect. Gray, at a shade over six feet, didn't consider himself short, but Brazier towered above him.

Gray gave Brazier a fast run-down of status, what little there was of it, while the CSM moved to the back of the van, opened the doors and extracted gloves, white evidence suit, face mask, and blue overshoes.

When Gray had finished, Brazier said, "Put these on." Like Gray needed telling.

Brazier turned to his forensics colleague, a young woman with braided hair and freckles across her cheeks, who he didn't bother to introduce. "Start a crime scene list, would you?"

The list would detail who'd accessed the property and when. Brazier and Gray would be at the top.

The double-fronted detached house was in shadow. High walls surrounded the premise like a medieval city fortification, but the metal barred gate was open, one of the sliding kind, wheels driven by electric motors. A red light high on the outside of the house indicated a burglar alarm. There was an intercom set to the right of the gate. It struck an odd note with Gray – this was a low crime, safe district. The security measures seemed a bit excessive, but, then again, the wealthy could sometimes be a bit overprotective of their assets.

Fowler was standing a few feet away. Gray walked over to him. "Mr Lavater mentioned the house is occupied by Mrs Usher. Is she related to Duncan Usher at all?"

"She's his wife."

"Bloody hell. That changes everything."

"Best call Copeland in."

Detective Chief Inspector Terry Copeland was Gray's boss, a brash and forthright man. The spider in the middle of CID's web.

"Have you called him yet?" asked Fowler.

"No."

Fowler sucked in his breath through a gap in his teeth. Copeland wanted to know everything that happened on his patch, as soon as it happened. Preferably before, if such a thing were possible. Murders were a rarity in Thanet, and Copeland insisted on being at the centre of every significant case.

"Considering Copeland has had a hard-on for Usher ever since he transferred here, I'd get on the blower immediately. Just my advice. Do what you think is best, though. After all, you're CID, I'm just the uniform grunt."

"No, you're right." Gray stepped a few paces away from Fowler, pulled his mobile out and dialled Copeland's number. His effort went through to voicemail.

"Sir, it's DC Gray. Can you call me as soon as you get this? It's very important." Gray disconnected. He hadn't felt comfortable giving Copeland any further information.

"No luck?" asked Fowler. Gray shook his head. "It's all yours then, for now. They don't come any bigger than Duncan Usher. Anything illegal going on in Thanet, you can bet Duncan's got a hand in it. This could be a big case, you lucky bastard."

"I'm not sure I'd use the word lucky."

Brazier approached the two. "Are you ready, Sol?"

"Coming."

"Break a leg," said Fowler.

Gray followed the CSM into the grounds of Valerie Usher's house. Gray's adrenaline was raised another notch; he tried to force his breathing down to a normal rate. He wiped damp palms on his trousers before pulling on nitrile gloves. He wished Jeff Carslake, his Sergeant, mentor, and friend, were here. Carslake would know what to do, he always did. Gray had attended major crime scenes in the past, but in uniform. Like Fowler, he'd stayed on the outside of the cordon, wishing he was inside. Well, now it was his turn. His first major case since joining CID less than a year ago.

But an Usher. *Don't screw this up.* Copeland would tear a strip off him if he made any sort of mistake. Copeland's style was to move hard and fast through an investigation, keeping his team on the balls of their feet. Gray had to take his time, be measured, miss nothing.

The drive was a large rectangular slab with sufficient room to park three or four cars, either side. Tree branches draped over the space, the leaves still in the stifling night air. The front door was, indeed, wide open, exposing a darkened hallway. At the entrance, Brazier stepped to the side and let Gray go ahead of him.

Gray paused for a couple of heartbeats. He looked over his shoulder. Fowler was watching. Fowler shooed Gray forward with a flap of his hands. The other forensics officer, the woman with the braids, was walking down the drive towards Gray and Brazier. Taking a deep breath, Gray crossed the threshold, Brazier in his wake, and fumbled for the light switch. A bright chandelier-style fitting lit the hall. More lights flickered on above the stairs and spilled down from the landing, reflecting off photo frames on the wall. Gray, Brazier, and his colleague split up to search the downstairs first.

Watching where he put his feet, Gray entered a large open-plan living–dining room. Wall-to-ceiling French windows looked out onto what he expected would be the back garden, though right now it was pitch black outside. Judging by the sofa cushions and curtains, the occupant clearly liked leopard skin.

Directly in the centre of the room was a large, ornate fire surround. Its rugged façade deviated from the rest of the home's modern interior decor, particularly the inset gas fire. Atop the surround were photos in silver frames. Gray studied several without picking them up. Children, twin girls, were in all of them, ageing steadily from left to right across the mantle. Growing up from tiny babies, side by side in incubators, to young girls older than Gray's own daughter. Maybe eight or nine?

Alongside photos of the girls were two grinning women with striking similarities; high cheekbones and green eyes, both with hair cut short – one bottle blonde, the other grey. *Mother and grandmother.*

Back in the hall, Gray found Brazier in conversation with a person filling the front entrance. It was Carslake, wearing an evidence suit. Gray felt a bite of relief that the crime scene would be Carslake's responsibility.

Carslake broke off from his conversation with the CSM and turned to Gray. "What have you found so far?"

"Not much. Nobody downstairs." He took Carslake into the lounge, showed him the photos. "It appears a mother and two daughters live here. Maybe the grandmother too." Gray paused. "She's Duncan Usher's wife."

"I know, and they're apparently estranged. Where's Copeland?"

"I've no idea. I called him straight away, but he didn't answer. I left a voice mail."

"Not much we can do if he won't pick up." Carslake turned and nodded to the stairs. "What about up there?"

"That was next."

The pair took the carpeted steps, Carslake a step ahead of Gray. There were more photos in frames leading upwards. The same family members. On the wide landing, all but one of the pale wooden doors were firmly shut. Two, to his right, each had pieces of paper taped to them, the names, Elodie and Lotty, surrounded by drawings.

"You check out the girls' rooms," said Carslake, heading in the other direction.

Gray put a palm on the nearest door handle, Elodie's, dreading what he might find. He pushed the door back, which moved smoothly on its hinges. The room was ordered but jumbled, the bed made up. Books were everywhere, on a freestanding shelf, in piles on the floor.

No one inside. Gray moved to Lotty's. To Gray's huge relief, her room was empty too; the bed also appearing to be unslept in. Posters on the walls, a guitar leaning haphazardly on a stand beneath the window. Several dolls lay on the floor as if they'd been discarded mid-play. Maybe the children were in the other room? Where Carslake had gone.

Gray crossed the landing to the room Carslake had entered, then paused in the doorway. The overhead light was on.

Floral curtains were drawn across a window on one side, a free-standing wardrobe and a matching set of drawers on the other. Above the bed was a large, framed photo of Mrs Usher with two young girls, the setting obviously staged in a studio. Gray recognised all three from the images downstairs.

Beneath the photo stood a substantial bed, king-size at least. On top of the mattress, a naked woman was sprawled out on her back, a pillow covering her face. The leopardskin duvet cover was rucked up in a pile on the floor. However, the bottom sheet was gone; the woman lay on what appeared to be a mattress topper. Gray assumed the sheet had been taken to remove evidence.

Carslake was crouched beside the bed. Gray moved closer; saw a man lying on the floor in a foetal position. He'd been concealed initially by the bed. A pool of dark blood, which had leaked from an outstretched arm, stained the cream-coloured carpet. Nearby was a long-bladed kitchen knife. His wrists were slashed. The man was young, slightly flabby, dressed in black shorts and an England football top. They seemed to be a matching set. His feet were bare. Carslake pressed two fingers into the man's neck.

Gray thought he saw his chest rise and fall slightly. "He's still alive." He could see blood leaking slowly from the man's wrists. Gray got his hands around them and squeezed, trying to stop the flow.

"There's an ambulance outside," said Carslake, "I'll get the paramedics." He ran out.

Gray continued to squeeze while he waited. Within a minute, a pair of green uniformed medics were at his side.

"We'll take it from here," said one. Gray rose and backed away, retreating onto the landing where he watched the medics work on the man, Carslake beside him, leaning on the bannister.

"I couldn't feel a pulse," said Carslake, shaking his head.

"He can't have come from far," said Gray, "he wasn't wearing anything on his feet. Do you recognise him?"

"Never seen him before." Carslake shook himself. "We need to carry on. Anything in the girls' rooms?"

"They're empty," said Gray. Carslake leaned inside Lotty's room, then Elodie's. Gray thought of his own family, his daughter, Hope, and son, Tom and shuddered once more.

"The beds haven't been slept in; maybe they're staying with friends or family?"

"I hope to God they are."

"We need to contact the next of kin."

"I'll get someone on it," Carslake said. "There's not much more we can do until the paramedics clear out. Go get some fresh air. You look like you're going to be sick any minute. And try Copeland again."

Gray nodded. He was grateful for the break. He headed outside, peeled off the gloves and overshoes, pausing a moment before pulling out his mobile and hitting redial. The call to the DI dropped into voicemail once more.

"Sir, DC Gray trying to reach you again. It's urgent you get in touch with me." Gray disconnected. If it had been anyone else, he wouldn't have bothered leaving another voicemail, but he wanted Copeland to know he'd made the effort.

Fowler and his uniformed colleagues had raised a cordon, keeping back a handful of onlookers who'd gathered to see what was going on. The street had filled considerably since he'd been inside. There were two more SOCO vans, the ambulance, and the pathologist, Dr Amos Jenkinson, a white-haired, blunt Northerner, well into his fifties, who sported pork-chop side-burns. He stood beside the freckled SOCO who was writing his name down on the crime-scene log.

Fowler came over. "How was it?"

"Unpleasant," said Gray, glad to be away from the blood.

"Want a beer later to help get over it?" Fowler had clearly got over his petulance.

"I think it's going to be a long night."

"All the more reason to go to the pub after," grinned Fowler.

"They'll be closed by the time we're done here. I've got to go." Gray made his way over to Jenkinson.

"Sol," said Jenkinson by way of greeting. "How many bod-ies?"

"One, a woman. And a man barely alive."

Carslake emerged from the house and joined them. "Para-medics have stabilised him. He's lost a lot of blood. We won't be talking to him for a while. If at all."

Just then the paramedics wheeled the man out on a stretch-er; the white bandages wrapped around his forearms a bright spot in the darkness. They loaded him into the ambulance. One of the PCs from the cordon joined the patient before the doors were closed and the ambulance pulled off.

"Right," said Jenkinson, rubbing his hands together, "let's get to work." He strode away.

"Did you catch Copeland?" asked Carslake.

"Voicemail again."

"He's not going to like being out of the loop."

"Don't I know it, Jeff. But if he's not answering what can I do?"

"Not a bloody thing."

Gray nodded, though he knew it was an excuse Copeland wouldn't accept. "I'll give Kate a quick call."

"Hurry it up, Sol."

Gray moved away from Carslake, rang home.

"I guess you're calling to say you'll be late again," said Kate, Gray's wife, when she answered.

"Sorry, love."

"What's going on?"

"I can't say, but it's serious. And I was first on the scene, so I have to see it through. How are the kids?"

"Asleep."

"Have you had a good day?"

"I'd have preferred it if I saw my husband occasionally."

Carslake was giving Gray a wind it up hand signal. "I've got to go. I'll see you when I see you."

"Please try and be quiet when you come in, Sol. I don't want you waking the children again."

"I'll try."

Gray disconnected and rejoined Carslake, who was talking to Fowler. "Mike, get a door-to-door going. I want to know if anyone saw something. Start with that lot hanging around at the cordon."

"Yes, sir."

"And we need a next of kin starting. Anyone else here from CID yet?"

"I'll go and see." Fowler scuttled off.

"How's Kate?" asked Carslake.

"Pissed off. How does your marriage work?"

"Basically, Sol, there are three choices. You both either come to live with it and stay married, you can't live with it and divorce, or you get another job."

"I can't imagine being without Kate or the job."

"Then you'll have to find a way."

Two

Now Two guards guided Duncan Usher up the concrete stairs to the prison governor's office. The one behind Usher had Blakey's on the heels of his shoes, metal protectors which clicked with every pace the man took. As they ascended the stairs, the prison stench receded – body odour, piss, over-boiled vegetables. It had been worse when smoking was allowed.

Usher didn't know what was going on – why he was being brought here. He hadn't met Governor Jones since his first days inside, when the governor had personally warned the new inmate not to cause any trouble. Jones knew he was dealing with Margate's kingpin, and he wanted to make certain Usher understood who was in charge now.

That had been fifteen years ago.

Fifteen years in which time Usher had battled his conviction from the inside while his lawyer fought from the outside. As long as he maintained his innocence, the opportunity to go in front of the parole board would be denied whenever he became eligible. According to the authorities, he was a killer, and convicted murderers were supposed to repent. Those who confessed their sins received the opportunity to return to "normal" life. Those who did not, remained trapped, serving their full sentence. So for Usher to be taken upstairs was highly unusual. Perhaps, at last, someone was beginning to listen to him.

They paused outside the wooden office. One guard unlocked Usher's handcuffs while the other knocked and then opened up without waiting for permission.

"Go on." Usher got a shove in the shoulder to emphasise the demand when he didn't immediatly move. Once he was inside, the door closed behind him, the guards remaining outside. But that wasn't the only revelation, because the man standing behind the desk was not Jones.

"Sit down," he gestured to the metal chair in front of Usher which was bolted to the floor. "I'm Smits."

Without answering, Usher took a seat. He kept his eyes firmly on the stranger, waiting to learn why they were both here. Smits had a bulbous head, a single stripe of hair along one side, the rest of the skull bald. And slightly bulging eyes.

Smits came around the front of the desk and perched on a corner. "I'd like your help." He crossed his arms. No preamble. "In return you'll get your freedom."

Usher narrowed his eyes. *What kind of ploy was this?* The scepticism must have flitted across his face because Smits smiled.

"I don't care who you are," said Usher, "I just want to know what you are."

"I'm the conscience of the police. I suspected you wouldn't trust me, so I've had a letter drawn up, laying out my commitment. It's been reviewed by your lawyer, here's a letter confirming that to be fact." Smits slid a document across the desk.

Usher leaned in, read the note where it lay, sat back. "That's Dowling's signature."

Smits followed with another piece of paper, placing it next to the first. Usher got closer again, read slowly. The contents were an offer, giving Usher what he'd always wanted. His innocence.

Something smelt about all of this, thought Usher. He said, "Why now?"

"I asked the guards to take off your shackles in a gesture of good faith. I hope you appreciate that?"

Usher noticed Smits had answered his question like a politician: dealing with a question by posing another. "Where's Jones?"

"It's best we keep this matter private. You'll see one of the clauses is a non-disclosure statement." Smits stuck a finger on a paragraph. "In other words, should you sign all aspects of the agreement, the contents will be confidential. If you break this clause, you'll be straight back in prison, serving the rest of your original sentence."

"I'm really being released?" Usher struggled to keep the eagerness out of his voice. After years of fighting, at last.

But Usher wasn't a trusting man. His original doubts cast a shadow over his elation. He needed to know exactly what Smits got out of this. "My lawyer is close to getting me out anyway."

"Close is one thing. This moves you to the other side of the gates in a matter of weeks. Guaranteed. Your lawyer will take considerably longer. That's if he even succeeds. How many setbacks have you had over the years?"

Plenty.

"What's in this for you?" asked Usher.

"My role is to root out corruption in the police force. I want to bring someone down. With your cooperation. And it relates to the death of your wife."

Usher gripped the arms of the chair. "Who?"

THE SAME GUARDS RETURNED Usher to his cell. On the way back, Usher thought about what was next. It had been a no-brainer to sign. Better the fresh air than the stink of incarceration.

When the steel door clanged behind him, Usher gave the guards a couple of minutes to clear off before he pulled the phone out from its hiding place behind the toilet cistern. It was an iPhone 4, not entirely up to date but sufficiently smart for what he needed and narrow enough to squeeze into a tight space. Officially Usher was allowed one call a week on the prison landlines, which were monitored, of course. Other than Frank McGavin, there was nobody for him to ring. His ex-mother-in-law wouldn't speak to him and neither would his daughters.

Usher turned the phone on, and the Apple logo illuminated the screen. Security was surprisingly lax when it came to mobile communication in prison. Many of the cons had phones and were able to continue their enterprises from inside. Usher was amazed that wireless blockers hadn't been established. As usual, reception was three bars.

Frank McGavin was a careful man. He only used unregistered burners and just once. Each time they communicated, McGavin ended with the details of the next burner's number, which Usher stored into the iPhone's memory.

Usher hit dial.

McGavin answered within a handful of rings. "Duncan, how's things?"

"I'm getting out, Frank."

"No shit? That's great news! When?"

"Twenty-four to forty-eight hours. I'll need picking up."

"Of course, I'll have Telfer do it. We'll have a party, celebrate your release."

"No, Frank, not yet. When I know for sure which one of the three of them framed me, then we'll tear it up."

"Sounds good to me."

"As soon as I have a time of release, I'll let you know via the official channels."

McGavin laughed. "Come to the restaurant. I'll make sure you get a decent meal."

"Perfect. One more thing, though."

"Anything. Just ask."

"I need a couple of numbers. For Carslake and Copeland. I'm going to give them the good news."

McGavin laughed once more. "I love it. But what about Gray?"

"I'm going to deal with him face-to-face. Keep them on their toes a bit."

"I'll text you the details. Carslake is still here, but Copeland has retired up north."

"Thanks Frank, for everything."

"No need. I'll see you soon." McGavin disconnected.

A moment later his phone vibrated twice in quick succession. The new burner number and Carslake's. Copeland's would follow once McGavin had it.

In contrast, Carslake answered immediately.

"Hello?" Carslake sounded distracted. Usher hadn't heard his voice for years. "Hello?"

"Chief Inspector," said Usher. "How are you?"

"Who is this?" Puzzled now.

"You mean after all this time you've forgotten me? Now that's just plain rude."

"It's been a long day."

"Well, we can make our acquaintance again soon, because I'll be getting out."

"Out?"

"From where you put me. This time you can't stop it happening. The wheels of justice are in motion. In just a few days we'll be able to shake hands again. I thought you'd like to know."

Carslake paused on the other end of the line, as if clicking through memories. Eventually he said, "Duncan? Duncan Usher?"

"The one and only. I knew you wouldn't let me down. Well, not again anyway."

"You're being released?"

"Jeff, you're being particularly slow today. That's what I said. And I'll be coming home. First person I'll be having a word with is Solomon Gray. I'm sure he'll be very interested to hear what I have to say."

"What about?"

"His lad, Tom, of course. I'll be seeing you soon, Jeff. And it's not going to be pretty. Count on it."

The line went dead. Carslake must have cut the call. Usher smiled to himself. He powered down the phone and concealed it once more before lying down on his bunk. Today had been a litany of unexpected events.

Usher had been surprised by Smits's revelation, though. If he'd drawn up a list of the most corrupt cops he'd met, Terry Copeland's name would have been right at the top.

Not Solomon Gray's.

Three

N^{ow} Solomon Gray stretched out the aches in his body. So far the train journey had taken six-and-a-half hours. Nearly five hundred miles north, from Broadstairs to Edinburgh via London in a carriage that reeked of stale coffee and bacon sandwiches.

If he'd driven, Gray would be lucky to have made it two thirds of the way by now, given the level of traffic on the roads these days. And the major thoroughfare to Edinburgh along the east coast dropped to a single lane just beyond Newcastle, slowing progress even further.

But the major factor was Gray's cancer; driving was no longer an option. He tired quickly as the chemotherapy nearly sapped the life out of him, of all the ironies. Afterwards, Gray never quite got back to where he started in terms of vigour and vitality. It was like his reserves were chipped away each time, and he was never able to fully replenish them. Just a few months to go, though, and his doctor seemed pleased with the progress he was making.

Nor could he ask for a lift (though Fowler had offered) as Gray was keeping news of his illness to himself, calling in sick or taking holidays when needed. So far he had managed, but he wondered how. He'd lost some weight, and his clothes hung off him. Perhaps it was because his colleagues were used to him looking like death warmed up. This time they were closer to the mark than they realised.

When the train halted, Gray remained seated. He packed away the travel chess set he'd brought with him to while away the time. He'd started playing recently and had a larger set at home on the coffee table. He waited for everyone else to disembark, avoiding the rush to the exit which started when the train began to slow. A bearded businessman was blocking the automatic door between the carriages, which kept attempting to close on him; such was his eagerness to exit the rubbish-strewn carriage.

Once the aisle was clear, Gray lifted down his quilted jacket and a small, black wheeled suitcase from the rack above. He'd packed a few clothes and some toiletries, enough for a couple of days. If all went well, and he decided to stay longer, there were plenty of shops to buy clothes from. But, as usual, he erred towards the side of pessimism.

He stepped down onto the platform, welcomed the chill blast of air through Edinburgh's historic Waverley Station. There was a noticeable temperature difference between here, due west from central Denmark, and Thanet from where you could see Belgium and Holland on a clear day with binoculars.

Gray made his way through the concourse, filled with light from the curved glass ceiling above, dodging fellow striding travellers on seemingly urgent journeys. A knot of people stood around the huge destinations and departures board.

Waverley was conveniently located in the city; a set of stairs brought him up onto the busy thoroughfare of Princes Street. For once, Gray had splurged, booking the Balmoral, an imposing Victorian five-star hotel adjacent to the station. The building looked like a castle, albeit with a large, central clock tower. After a brief glance upwards Gray headed for the entrance, keeping his bag close to heel. Within, a concierge, dressed in a neat three-piece suit, nodded a greeting at Gray as he passed.

The entrance lobby was dominated by a wide, striped carpet and several large palms whose presence gave the area a colonial feel. The air was clean and the surroundings felt hushed after the confines and activity of the train. Gray was checked in by a smiling young woman, accepted a key card but turned down both the access to the hotel spa and the besuited bellboy's offer to carry his bag. He stepped into the lift and pressed the "4" button. Room 417 was full of light and pleasantly warm. A throw across the king-sized bed had the same striping as the lobby carpet. Gray dumped his bag before looking out the window. His view was onto the garden and the monument to Sir Walter Scott, just along Princes Street. People went about their business beneath him.

Gray returned to the bed, unzipped his case and pulled out a small vanity bag. Rather than toiletries it was filled with small brown plastic bottles, neatly labelled, identifying the drugs Gray had to swallow each day to combat his cancer. He unscrewed the cap on several bottles, tipped a capsule from one after the other into the palm of his hand and went into the bathroom. He threw the handful of pills down his throat, drew a glass of water, and swallowed. He caught sight of himself in the mirror. His face was gaunt, black bags under his eyes.

"You look like shit, Sol," he murmured to himself.

Nothing he'd packed would benefit from being hung up on hangers, so he headed back outside to stretch his legs. He couldn't manage anything too strenuous, but sitting cooped up in his room wouldn't do. His gut was tied up in knots. It had been nine years. *Would he recognise her? Could she ever forgive him?* In just a few hours, he'd finally get to see his daughter, Hope, again.

HOPE'S SUGGESTED MEETING place was a busy Italian restaurant crammed with tables and young families, not far from the Balmoral. He arrived early and was taken to his seat by a waiter with what sounded like an authentic Italian accent. The waiter leaned over the table and lit a red candle stuck into an old bottle covered in wax drips. Gray ordered water. A basket of bread arrived, he buttered and ate it while he waited, staring out the window.

The minutes ticked by. Gray checked his watch. Hope was late. He had no idea if that was normal for her or not. His phone was lying on the table. No messages. Gray checked for the third time. The waiter came over, eyebrows raised.

"She'll be here soon," said Gray. He received a mildly pitying look in response, obviously the man assumed Gray had been stood up by his date. Which was partially true. Gray's phone beeped – a text from Hope.

"I'm sorry, Dad," it read. "I can't do this. I'm not ready. So sorry. Please give me more time."

Gray's stomach plunged with disappointment. He put the phone down and dropped his head to his hands.

"Is she not coming?" asked the waiter, his accent now Scottish.

Feeling his face colour Gray lied, "She's ill."

"Look, no rush. If you want to stay, you're welcome. If you want a proper drink, just let me know."

"Thanks."

The waiter departed. Gray picked up his mobile and was about to call Hope until he realised that would probably only push her away. He read the message again. It implied they'd meet at some point, which Gray took some heart from. He pulled a ten pound note out of his wallet, threw it on the table, and left as quickly as he could.

As he stepped outside his mobile rang. *Maybe she's changed her mind?* But no, it was Carslake, probably to see how it was going with Hope. Gray sent it to voicemail. A moment later Carslake rang again. Once more, Gray rejected it, this time switching the phone off and going for a walk.

Anywhere.

GRAY WAS SITTING NEAR the Scott Monument in Princes Street Gardens. He'd been here for half an hour or more. It was drizzling. His brown hair was plastered to his forehead. The rain was soaking through his jacket, and he didn't have a hood. His backside was cold, and the sanctuary of the Balmoral was only yards away, but he didn't care.

The disappointment at not seeing Hope weighed like a brick on his chest. He turned his mobile back on to see if she had changed her mind. Immediately a string of texts from Carslake buzzed through, all asking where he was and telling him to call ASAP. The texts got shorter and blunter as they progressed.

Gray dialled, and Carslake picked up immediately.

"Where the hell have you been?"

"Edinburgh."

"That's not what I meant; I've been trying to get hold of you."

"I'm on leave, Jeff."

"I know. This is important, though. I wouldn't have rung otherwise. Have you seen the news today?"

"I haven't had the chance."

"Then take a look and call me back right away."

"What's going on?"

"You'll know when you see it."

Gray disconnected, puzzled.

BACK IN HIS HOTEL ROOM, Gray changed the television channel to the twenty-four-hour BBC news feed. A politician was on screen, making some self-absorbed claim which Gray couldn't be bothered to hear. He muted the sound, relying on the ticker tape at the bottom as it scrolled across the screen. Gray peeled off his clammy jacket and hung it over a chair. He grabbed a towel from the bathroom and was vigorously rubbing his hair when he saw it. Gray paused, his dampness forgotten.

Convicted murderer Duncan Usher released from prison after alleged miscarriage of justice.

At the top of the hour, Gray turned on the sound. Usher was the lead story. A female newsreader with blonde hair, black eyebrows, and a wrinkle-free forehead which spoke of either superb genes or botox, stared seriously into the camera lens.

"Earlier today Duncan Usher, found guilty fifteen years ago of his wife's murder, was released from Wandsworth Prison," she said. "Our reporter is in south-west London to give us the full story."

The view cut to a balding man clutching a microphone, his coat open at the neck to expose a shirt and tie. He was standing across from the prison gates, a road in between with cars passing by from side to side. The reporter maintained an equally stern expression and spoke loudly to be heard above the traffic.

"Two hours ago, Duncan Usher, a man until today serving life for murder, attempted murder, and perverting the course of justice, was set free, stepping outside for the first time in a decade and a half."

Footage of Usher getting into a car and speeding away cut in before switching back once more to the reporter.

"As yet there has been no official reason given for his release, but the BBC understands evidence has come to light, which casts doubt on his original conviction."

Another change of scene brought up archive footage of the house where Usher's dead wife had been found, and the start of yet another telling of the grisly tale. Gray had lived it once already, he didn't need to hear it all again. He muted the TV. He thought the case was long done and buried deep. No wonder Carslake had been agitated. Gray felt sick. The ghosts of the past would be stirring now.

Gray rang Carslake back.

"YOU'VE SEEN IT THEN," said Carslake. "The lawyers are claiming a false conviction. Poor procedure and a corrupt investigation."

"They're right."

"You need to come back to Margate."

"I know."

Carslake paused before asking, "How did it go with Hope?"

"It didn't."

"What do you mean?"

"She didn't turn up."

"I'm sorry."

"So am I. Anyway, it can't be helped. I'll catch the first train back in the morning."

"Good, I'll see you then."

Gray called down to reception, told them he'd be checking out in the morning, as something had unexpectedly come up. The person he spoke to was understanding. No howls of protest about a visit cut short. Gray hadn't even unpacked and already he was leaving. This wasn't how he'd foreseen the trip.

Next, he looked up train times for the following day. The ticket he'd bought restricted when he could travel, and there weren't any seats available until after 9 a.m. The route was direct to London, meaning business travellers heading in for early morning meetings.

Gray felt he had to tell Hope. He retrieved her text and sent a reply, saying he completely understood. He added that he had to go back to Margate tomorrow morning on police business. He hated saying that, it felt like history repeating itself to the detriment of his relationships. He and his wife Kate had argued often over the demands of the job. But it was true, and he wasn't going to lie to his daughter. He sent the message.

The TV caught Gray's attention. Usher was on screen. From the multitude of microphones on the table in front of him, it was clear he was giving a press conference.

It was the first time Gray had seen him since sentence had been passed. Usher's face, and hair, had thinned a bit, but otherwise he hadn't changed much. He still appeared the confident, self-assured person Gray had known. Gray picked up the remote and turned the sound on, Usher was apparently now taking questions.

"How does it feel to be free after all these years?" asked a female reporter from out of shot.

Usher narrowed his eyes, taking a moment to consider an answer. "My wife is dead. I'm estranged from my daughters, who've grown up believing a lie. I've got a grandchild I don't know, I've been wrongfully imprisoned for years, and officially I'm still a convicted murderer. So, in answer to your question. It's great to be out, but I'm not free."

"But that conviction will now be quashed?" asked the same reporter.

"I'm hoping so. First we have to get to the truth, to find out what really happened to Valerie."

"And what did happen, Mr Usher?"

"It was the police. They set me up." Usher stared at the camera. Gray felt as if he were looking right at him, as they had across an interview table when Usher had first been brought in. "Now, if you will excuse me," said Usher, "I have a pint waiting for me at the bar."

Usher stood and left the room to a buzz of conversation. A man opened a door for him and followed him through. The view was only fleeting, but he looked like Dean Telfer – though bald now and minus the jewellery Usher's right-hand man wore back in the day.

Gray switched off the television. He headed to the minibar and searched through the bottles. *Whisky.* When in Scotland and all that. He shouldn't drink, but he didn't care. He poured the shot into a glass, dribbled in a tiny amount of water from the tap and sat in front of the window, looking out over the city, knowing that whatever tomorrow brought, it would not be welcome.

Four

Then Duncan Usher peeled the bloody gloves from his hands. He inspected his knuckles, ignoring the bubbling sobs from behind him. His skin was clean. No signs he'd just beaten a man half to death. His shirt was spattered though. Usher would need to change it before he emerged.

It hadn't been a fair fight. The other guy was bound to a chair, no chance of defending himself, never mind fighting back. Usher crossed to a sink, washed his hands and dried them carefully. Usher liked to be clean.

"What do you want to do with him?" asked Frank McGavin, one of the closest of Usher's few confidantes. Usher turned around.

McGavin might have appeared soft, but he was far from it. Thin and well-dressed in expensive clothes, McGavin was not one to underestimated. His greatest asset was his mind. He was sharp, fast to plot several courses of action from a given start point and assess the consequences. He'd risen far and fast with Usher.

With McGavin was Dean Telfer, Usher's driver. Usher didn't use bodyguards, bad for the image. Telfer though, an ex-boxer, could handle himself and others. He was short, with slicked back hair. He wore a chain round his neck and several large rings on the fingers of both hands. They came in handy sometimes when people needing some "convincing". Both his ears were pierced with gold hoops. Telfer gave off an edge, one of repressed menace. His eyes were always on the move, expecting trouble.

The pair stood either side of the beaten man who was leaning forward in the chair, only held upright by the ropes. Blood and saliva dripped from his battered face onto the floor. The mess would be hardly noticeable.

They always used a garage for this kind of work, where the smell of spilled oil and fuel masked everything. Some sawdust on the floor, a quick sweep up, and it was all just another workshop stain. And there were plenty of tools on hand. Pliers, hammers, even a blow torch should the interviewee prove particularly resistant. It was unusual for Usher himself to do the work, but this one had crossed over the line, taken from his boss and blamed someone else. Transgressions like that had to be dealt with, visibly.

"Get rid of him at sea," said Usher. It was the easiest way. Load the man onto a fishing boat in the dead of night, chug out a couple of miles, fix some weights to his legs with chains and a padlock, and the corpse would never be found. Fish food.

Telfer's phone rang. He listened briefly, lifted his eyes to Usher, disconnected. "That was the cops," he said. "It's Valerie."

"What's the stupid cow done now?" asked Usher. "I swear to God, if she wasn't the mother of my children," Usher scrunched his fingers into fists again, tempted to swing one more time at the battered man.

"She's dead."

Usher paused, arm mid-arc. "How?"

"I don't know. She was found at her home."

"The cops will want to speak with you," said McGavin.

"Obviously," said Usher, aware he couldn't use his current whereabouts and activity as an alibi. "Frank, get this mess sorted. Dean, take me home."

Five

Now Gray wasn't ready to leave Edinburgh, but he had to. He zipped his case closed, took the lift downstairs, and handed in his key card. After returning the receptionist's best wishes for the day, Gray crossed the lobby, stepped onto the street, and stopped in his tracks.

A young woman stood on the pavement, staring intently at him. She was so familiar it ached. So much like Kate, Gray's deceased wife; tall, slim, and with long brown hair. Neither of them moved for a few moments, the rest of the world rushing on without them. Gray closed the gap, paused a foot away, not sure what to do next, standing a full head in height above her.

"*Daddy, it's really you!*" Hope threw her arms around her father, buried her head in his chest. She began to cry.

Solomon Gray slowly enveloped his daughter as his own tears began to flow.

"WHEN IS YOUR TRAIN due?" asked Hope. She stirred sugar into a cup of coffee. Gray was surprised. Kate hadn't allowed the children sugar in drinks. However, Hope had spent the last few years with her grandparents and then on her own. Different influences.

"The earliest is just after 9 a.m., but I've got a flexible ticket, so I can leave on pretty much any."

Hope checked her watch. "Not long then."

"If I decide not to take that one, we've got some time."

Gray took a sip of his flat white. It was decent. Often baristas got it wrong, made them more like a latte, the extra milk overpowering the bitterness of the bean.

"I'm sorry about yesterday." She kept her eyes on the revolving spoon. Gray noticed she wore a silver chain round her neck, a cross hanging from it, a design very similar to one of her mother's. "I just panicked; I wasn't sure what I'd say to you."

"I understand. How many years has it been?" Gray knew exactly and to the month.

"Too many." Hope peered at Gray. "Are you all right?"

"I'm fine, I always look like this," lied Gray. "And it doesn't matter now, because you're here. What changed your mind?"

Hope raised her head and smiled at Gray. There was genuine warmth within. She put the spoon on the table. "My boyfriend. He said I shouldn't let you leave without at least attempting to speak to you. We may never have got another opportunity. He called the hotel to see if you'd left. I was on my way in when you came out."

"He sounds sensible. What's his name?"

"Hamish. He's a local if you hadn't guessed."

Gray laughed, Hope joined in. She became serious again. "Hamish was estranged from his father. He'd had an alcohol problem, pretended he had cancer, stuff like that. Really it was a cry for help."

Gray wasn't convinced; it sounded more like a cry for attention. And Gray was struck by the irony. One person fabricating an illness, and here he was keeping an actual disease secret.

Hope continued, "Anyway, Hamish's father died last year. He was discovered in his flat by the cleaner. He'd been dead for three days and no one had even noticed."

"Bloody hell."

"Awful, isn't it? That someone can become so distant from their family, that they don't even know he's passed. So Hamish told me not to make the same mistake."

"Mistake?"

"To not try. We might have hated each other, but at least we'd have known."

"No lingering regrets."

"Hopefully not."

"So far I don't hate you."

"So far?" Hope laughed.

"I've faith in us."

"Me too." Hope paused before saying, "Are you sure you're all right, Dad? You look worn out."

"I'm fine, just busy at work." Gray had been planning to tell her about his cancer, but he decided now wasn't the time, particularly after her revelation about Hamish's father. If Hope was going to stay in touch, it must be because she wanted to, not because she felt obligated. He changed the subject. "How's university?"

"Great. Hard work, but I love it."

"Nursing, right? That must be very rewarding."

"Helping people is what life's all about, isn't it?"

"Yes, even at a personal cost." Hope paused, put her hand out across the table. "I get that now, Dad." Gray covered her hand with his.

"How did you and Hamish meet?"

"At the hospital."

"Student or patient?"

"Neither, he's a consultant."

Which would make Hamish a lot older than Hope. Gray kept the voice inside his head locked up.

"Hopefully we can meet one day."

"We'd like that." Hope checked her watch. "Don't you need to go?"

"Probably."

"I'll walk with you to the station."

"Best not, otherwise I won't be leaving."

They exited the café, standing awkwardly outside. Gray wasn't sure what to do next. "I'm headed this way." Hope pointed in the opposite direction to where Gray needed to be. "Please come back again."

"I will."

"Promise?"

"I promise."

Hope gave Gray another big hug, followed by a kiss on the cheek.

"Bye, Dad. Love you." Then she was gone.

The train was well underway, snaking along the coast back towards Berwick and England. The trolley had just been past. Gray had taken a coffee, but it was swamp water compared to the stuff he'd drunk half an hour earlier in the café with Hope. It had tasted fine yesterday. He thought back over the conversation with his daughter and smiled. It had been brief but gone well, better than he could have wished for. Her final words were still a surprise to him. He touched the place on his cheek where Hope had kissed him.

He'd definitely be returning to Edinburgh, and soon.

Six

N^{ow} Gray was shattered by the time he arrived at the Margate police station. He almost nodded off in the swaying taxi, even though it was only a brief drive along the seafront.

"Bloody journalists," said the driver, jerking Gray out of the beginnings of a doze. "They're almost as bad as the politicians." All Gray could see of the driver was the back of his balding head and large ears.

A BBC TV van was parked in front of the station. Which meant reporters would be camping out there. "Can you take me round the back, please," said Gray.

"Okay, mate. Don't like the press either?"

"Not really."

"I don't know anyone who does."

There was indeed a huddle of journalists, talking among themselves while they awaited the news to happen before them. One or two turned towards the taxi as it drove past, but the glance was brief and uninterested.

In the car park, Gray paid the driver, collected his case from the boot, and went inside. He headed for the Detectives' Office, a collection of desks in a large open plan where he and his colleagues carried out the administrative aspects of the role, which were many.

Gray opened the office door to a commotion. Detective Sergeant Mike Fowler was flying his mini remote-control helicopter around the office again. He'd had it a few weeks, a birthday present or something. Whoever had purchased it was an idiot. The bloody thing was a menace in Fowler's hands, and, so far, Detective Inspector Yvonne Hamson had let the problem ride.

He watched Fowler fiddling with the controls like a giddy schoolboy. Hell, he even looked like a schoolboy now, his top lip naked after having recently shaved off his legendary pornstar moustache. Gray ducked as the drone buzzed over his head. Which was the point. Fowler wanted to be annoying. To push Hamson. A few faces looked to Gray, imploring him to do something. Gray's own relationship with Hamson was problematic, too. Recently they'd had a falling out in the staff canteen, and, since then, Hamson's demeanour towards him had remained chilly. Publicly tackling Fowler would hardly help.

However, Gray had no need. Hamson threw her pen onto her desk and stood up, a commanding six feet. Fowler, eyes focused on the helicopter, didn't notice her approach. She snatched the controller from his hands. *Thud.* The drone dropped to the floor. Surprise registered on Fowler's face, then shock when Hamson marched over to the helicopter, turned to meet Fowler's dumbfounded gaze, then pressed her patent shoe down hard enough to shatter the toy with a loud snap. Hamson scooped the larger pieces off the floor and dumped them into Fowler's lap along with the controller, then gave her blonde hair a careless toss as she returned to her desk.

Gray felt someone behind him. He glanced over his shoulder. Carslake. Catching sight of his DCI, Fowler bit back whatever he'd been planning to bark at Hamson.

"Briefing in the Major Incident Room. Two minutes," said Carslake and withdrew.

Silently the CID team filed out. Gray dropped his bag at his desk and followed his colleagues.

The Major Incident Room was used for precisely its namesake. It was similar to the Detective's Office; rectangular with a high ceiling. However, the dominant features were an expansive whiteboard, known as the murder board, where all information pertinent to a case was summarised, and a large, wall-mounted flat screen television. A couple of meeting rooms branched off to the side. Tables and chairs, lined up to face the whiteboard, filled the central space.

Right now the whiteboard was blank. Gray wasn't surprised to see the area commander, Superintendent Douglas Marsh standing before it, facing into the room. He was suited and booted in uniform. His cap lay on the nearest table. Marsh had silver hair and a hook nose. His bearing was upright, hands behind his back, chest pushed out in an attempt to convey strength and control. Gray knew all too well this was front because Marsh was a blusterer; used to getting his own way, and pissy when he didn't.

Marsh stood between Carslake and the station's Press Officer, Bethany Underwood. Underwood was tall, skinny and had frizzy bleached blonde hair, thinning because she'd applied the chemicals too often. She always seemed to be running on the edge – tense and stressed. Today was no exception, but at least she wasn't gnawing away at her cuticles for once.

Gray was last in, and he closed the door behind him. For once, there was little chat between the officers. They knew what this was about. Fowler stood near Gray, a female detective constable between them. Fowler leaned around the woman and scowled at Gray, presumably still smarting from having his toy smashed, before returning his attention to the senior management.

"The reason for bringing you all here," said Marsh, without preamble, "is the release of Duncan Usher. I'm unable to share all the details, but, what I can say is, new information has come to light which appears to prove his innocence. I'm sure you've noticed a gaggle of reporters outside. My presence here is to impress upon you the importance of presenting a united front to the press and public on what is and will remain a high profile and very sensitive case.

"It is critical we maintain consistent messaging. So if any of you are approached by a member of our esteemed press, direct them to Miss Underwood here." Marsh pointed towards Underwood who looked surprised to be addressed, jerking upright like a child caught in the act of doing something they shouldn't. "Your uniformed colleagues are being given the same message.

"Let me be clear," continued Marsh, "that is an order. If I learn anyone, from DI Carslake down, has been straying from this line, then we will implement disciplinary measures. And before anyone asks, it is not because I want to cover something up – just the opposite." Marsh fixed the room with a steely glare.

"Now, I am expecting two investigators from the Independent Police Complaints Commission to arrive at this station within the next day. Their task will be to conduct an investigation into the events of fifteen years ago. Not all of you worked here at that time. Those who did will be interviewed by the investigative team. You will be open, frank, and honest with them. Do I make myself understood?"

Fowler put his hand up.

"You're not at school anymore, Mike," said Carslake. Nervous laughter rippled around the room.

"Could prosecutions result from the IPCC's work?" asked Fowler.

"At this stage it's impossible to say," said Marsh. "The lead investigator may consider anyone a witness. However, our focus should not be on the IPCC. They simply have a job to do. We've nothing to hide and have done nothing wrong.

"Duncan Usher has always protested his innocence in the murder of his wife. If it's proven that Usher was wrongfully convicted, then we didn't catch the actual perpetrator back then. They need bringing to justice. Whoever they are. Any more questions?" He waited for just a few seconds. "No? Okay, I'll leave you all with DI Carslake." Marsh nodded at nobody in particular and left the room.

Carslake said, "I've nothing additional to add other than I support Superintendent Marsh. Please remember, any and every external enquiry gets referred to Bethany, okay?"

From the number of people dipping their heads in response from all around the room it was clear the message had got through. "If you've got any burning questions, see me or DI Hamson. Otherwise, back to your day jobs, please. Don't let Duncan Usher get in the way unless he has to."

The gathering broke up. "Sol," said Carslake, "a word if you don't mind."

Gray made his way over, heading in the opposite direction to everyone else, like a salmon swimming upstream.

Carslake allowed the room to empty and for the door to be closed before he said, "We need to talk, though not now and not here. What are you doing tonight?"

"I was intending to get some sleep. It's been a long day."

"Of course, stupid of me. What happened with Hope? You said she didn't turn up."

"Actually in the end it went really well." Gray heard the note of surprise in his own voice. "We had a little time together, after all."

"Good, I'm glad to hear it. But this can't wait. If the IPCC do arrive tomorrow, we need to have had a conversation first."

"Okay."

"Give me half an hour to clear my diary, and we'll go out for coffee. I'm buying." Carslake patted Gray on the arm before he left. "Everything will be fine."

Gray wondered why Carslake had felt the need to say that.

Regardless, Gray didn't trust Carslake a millimetre.

Seven

T hen
"You can come inside." Sean Brazier beckoned Gray and Carslake from the front door. The CSM held out fresh white suits and accompanying paraphernalia.

Once they were dressed, Gray and Carslake followed Brazier upstairs into the bedroom where the pathologist Jenkinson hovered just over the threshold. Valerie's lifeless body lay exactly where Gray had first seen her, though now she was bathed in tungsten white from overhead spotlights erected by SOCO to prevent shadows. Her skin was almost lost against the white mattress she was lying on. Her hands and feet were encased in plastic bags to protect any evidence that might be under her nails or on the skin. The pillow had been removed from her face. It would have been bagged also.

Her hair was short and blonde, the kind of platinum yellow which came from a bottle. Her flawless skin was accentuated with high cheekbones. Some people paid big money for such looks. Her eyes were closed, mouth open. Her lips were red with lipstick, matching the colour of her nails – both hands and feet. It was the same woman from the photographs, albeit with a different hair style.

"Nasty," said Brazier.

"Do you mean her or the scene?" asked Carslake.

"The scene of course, Jeff. It was just a remark."

"Unless they're pertinent to the case, keep them to yourself, Sean," snapped Carslake.

"My apologies," said Brazier.

Carslake turned his back on Brazier. "What do you think, Amos?"

Jenkinson sucked in a lungful of air through his teeth, ready to deliver a pronouncement in his Yorkshire accent. "Mrs Usher most likely died from strangulation. I'll determine the exact cause of death when I get a closer look, however from the marks around her neck, I'd say it's a good bet. I'll know for sure when I open her up and take a look at her larynx. If it's cracked or broken, then strangulation will be a certainty."

"Not asphyxiation from the pillow?" asked Gray.

"Doubtful, I would say, based on the signs."

"So why place the pillow over her face?"

"Shame, maybe? I'd suggest the killer closed her eyes too," said Jenkinson. "She'd have been staring right at him while he squeezed."

Carslake broke into the silence. "What about the attempted suicide?"

"Who says it's a suicide?"

"The slashed wrist is a strong indicator."

"Maybe, maybe not."

"We didn't find a suicide note," said Brazier. "There was this knife beside the bed." He passed over the bloodied weapon, which was inside a sealed evidence bag.

"Where specifically?" asked Carslake.

Brazier pointed to a large patch of blood on the carpet. "Beneath the man."

"Looks like it's from a kitchen." Carslake passed it to Gray. He looked at the weapon through the plastic. Gray had to agree. A black handle and a short, sharp blade.

"So maybe he strangled Valerie, then feeling remorse, went downstairs and got the knife. He sat on the floor, cut his wrists and lay down to bleed out," suggested Carslake.

"It's possible. Although there's one problem." Jenkinson was frowning. "I estimate the time of death to be around 10 p.m."

"He would have bled out within that time," said Gray.

"Yes."

"Unless he killed her, calmed down, then felt guilty and decided to kill himself?"

"It's a theory." Jenkinson sounded doubtful, though.

"There doesn't appear to be any sign of a forced entry," said Brazier.

"These two knew each other then?" suggested Carslake.

"It's possible," said Gray. "Thanet is a small area, and he wasn't wearing any shoes. He probably didn't come far."

"Can you prioritise the PM, Amos?" asked Carslake.

"She'll be at the top of the list."

"This was found beside the man." Brazier passed Carslake a mobile phone in a bag. "There's just one number on there. Says 'home'"

"Has anybody tried to call it yet?"

"So," a new voice interrupted. "Are any of you bastards going to fill me in on the good news?"

Gray turned; it was Copeland, their boss. And he looked ecstatic.

Eight

Now Gray met Carslake outside the station. It was bright and warm. Carslake was wearing sunglasses and had rolled up his shirt sleeves. Gray was the opposite. No shades, and he'd picked up his suit jacket in case there was a sea breeze. Instead it was dead calm. Gray was considering going back inside to dump his jacket, but Carslake got walking, leading them down Fort Road, which dropped away to the Margate seafront. Gray followed.

As they were passing the Turner Contemporary – a free-to-enter art gallery and a beacon of regeneration for the area, while barely giving a passing nod to the great artist himself – Carslake said, "There's cafés everywhere these days. More of them than pubs apparently, which is a bloody travesty. What about that one on the harbour arm?"

"Fine with me," said Gray.

The pair negotiated the road at a zebra crossing, strolled past the gallery and onto the jetty, a strip of concrete protecting the inner bay from the worst of the North Sea storms. A fistful of trawlers bobbed in its lee. Trawling was an endangered activity, like the fish they attempted to catch. Only one fishmonger in the whole area too. It was a modern tragedy of generational excess that an area which was three quarters coastline, received barely any fruits of the sea.

Squat structures stretched along the harbour arm, in the past they were used to process the day's catch. Gentrification was working its charms here, too. The dilapidated buildings had been made available by the council at a peppercorn rent simply so they were filled. One was a gallery run by a local artist on a very small scale, another was a bar, and finally there was the café. They entered. It was a little cooler inside, away from the sun.

Carslake ordered while Gray selected a squashy sofa. They were the only patrons. It was bare brick walls and quirky local marine memorabilia in a sterile nod to the past. Gray laid his jacket over the back of the seat. He settled into the softness of the cushions, tired from the journey and the effects of his treatment. Gray could easily fall asleep if he wasn't careful, so he stood up and glanced over the faux adornments while awaiting his drink.

After a few minutes, Carslake came over with a tray. "I got us some cakes too." Carslake sat down in an armchair on the opposite side of the table and pointed at the sweet treats. "Which one do you want?"

"I'm not bothered."

Carslake picked up an eclair and munched on one end. Cream squished out of the sides. Carslake used a finger to rescue the blob. Gray didn't fancy the doughnut Carslake had left.

"You said Edinburgh went well, Sol."

"Not at first, Hope didn't turn up. But she came to see me at the hotel this morning. We talked."

"That's great! You must be delighted."

"Of course. It means I'll be going back soon."

"Good." Carslake wiped his fingers on a napkin. "Have you got any plans for the weekend?"

"Nothing at the moment."

"I'm going to Dreamland with the grandkids now it's opened. Some big-name designer was involved in the refurb, yesteryear themed apparently. To drag more people down from the capital."

Gray had read that aspiration in the paper, however the locals were suitably negative about its prospects. As was Gray. "It'll fail," he said. Margate was more Beirut than Notting Hill, little to attract the casual visitor. He'd seen Londoners getting off the train to visit the gallery, wide-eyed at the grungy sights the town had to offer. He doubted many had returned. At least Dreamland was closer to the station. Fewer homeless drunks to bypass. "What's this clandestine stuff all about, Jeff?"

Carslake appeared taken aback. "Clandestine? Not at all, I just fancied getting out of the office."

"That wasn't the impression you gave me."

"Sorry, that wasn't my intent."

"I thought you'd want to discuss the IPCC investigation."

"I'm not overly concerned, to be honest."

"Really?"

"Did you do anything incorrect at the time?"

"No, but they're investigating a case I was integrally involved with."

"I think you're safe, you were a new DC at the time, after all. Copeland is who they'll really be looking at. And maybe me after him. I don't see you being identified as a person of interest."

"Who's they?"

"The senior investigator is someone called Eric Smits. He's going to be joined by Emily Wyatt."

"Do you know either of them?"

"Look Sol, leave the IPCC to me. I think your time would be far better spent on Hope. And Tom."

Gray leaned forward, suddenly energised. Carslake had found a witness who saw Tom being taken out of England into France on a ferry. Gray had finally met the man a few weeks ago but he'd been vague at best.

"Have you got some more information, Jeff?"

"Are you not having the doughnut?"

"Who gives a shit about a cake? Just tell me about Tom. Why are you holding out on me?"

Carslake shrugged and grabbed the doughnut. "First, I need you to understand the scale of the issue we're facing. Look at the Madeleine McCann disappearance. That was ten years ago. It's had all sorts of police resources thrown at it throughout the years and still nothing. Witnesses have moved on, others have died. Opportunity scattered to the wind. We're pretty much on our own when it comes to finding Tom. No massive resources and millions of pounds being thrown into the investigation. And we've an additional challenge in that no one considered the prospect of a European angle. He's a needle in a haystack, Sol. But even needles in haystacks can be found with enough effort, and I think I've got something."

Gray bent forward. His palms were damp but his mouth dry. He drank some coffee, his hands shaking a little, giving time for Carslake to fold half the doughnut into his mouth before Gray asked, "What, Jeff?"

"Initially Tom's trail petered out in Brussels, but signs indicate he went over the border, to Amsterdam. I'm following a series of potential sightings like breadcrumbs. Sometimes they disappear, and I have to search out the next one."

"Why didn't you tell me about this sooner, Jeff?"

"I wasn't sure it would turn out to be anything substantial, I'm still not. But now I'm going to be swamped by Smits so I want to pass everything over to you, okay?"

"It's time consuming."

"I don't care. I'll take the workload on." Gray would work all the spare hours he had if need be. It wouldn't be the first time.

"Good." Carslake drained his coffee. "How are things with Hamson?"

"Fine. Why wouldn't they be?"

Carslake stared at Gray for a moment. "They're clearly not, Sol. She can't stand to be in the same room as you."

"Just a misunderstanding. It'll work itself out. I'm not the easiest person to get on with."

"Don't blame yourself. Hamson seems unable to work well with anybody around her. Like Mike. That helicopter incident before the briefing." Carslake shook his head. "The whole office witnessed it."

Gray didn't know what to say that would make Carslake think better of Hamson, so he stayed quiet.

"Your silence does you credit, Sol. In your position many people would leap at the chance to criticise their superior. Many people have. When the Usher investigation is done and dusted, Hamson has to go."

Gray almost spat his coffee across Carslake. He swallowed then coughed. "That's a pretty drastic step, isn't it?" Gray wiped the back of his hand across his mouth.

"The atmosphere is terrible, you're aware of it. And this affair with Mike, it's unprofessional, frankly. Clearance rates are suffering, right at the worst possible moment when the IPCC are going to be all over me and Marsh. Hamson is the DI; she has to take responsibility for the problems."

"What about having a word with her?"

"God knows, I've tried." Carslake pulled a face like a child being offered unpalatable food.

"I didn't mean you. Human Resources."

"HR? God, no. They're a waste of space."

"You seem set on this, Jeff."

Carslake nodded emphatically. "I am."

Gray paused, let his mind roll. He picked up his coffee, but only the dregs remained. He placed the cup back in the saucer. "There has to be some other way. We're already short staffed."

"Believe me; I've spent a long time thinking it all through. Ideally I'd prefer her to put in a transfer request, one I couldn't refuse."

"And you want me to engineer it, I guess."

"You always were sharp, Sol."

"How am I going to do that?"

"Make friends with Hamson again, talk to her about her position."

Carslake seemed to have everything figured out. Gray said, "She might not be interested."

"Make her interested. Ideally I'd suggest moving Mike too, but I can't afford to lose both of them. And even though he's a pain the arse, at least he's a decent copper. However, if things carry on as they are and more complaints come in about Mike then then he could follow Hamson out the door."

"I've got to say, Jeff, I'm not comfortable with all this." Gray wondered what the real reason was for Carslake wanting to push out Hamson.

"I suspected you wouldn't be. You're too bloody straight, Sol. That's your problem. So, there's a potential direct benefit for you. With Hamson gone, an inspector's position frees up. Because of all your experience, it would be an obvious step. Think of it as a sweetener to sharpen the mind."

There it was, on the table before them. Hamson was to be the sacrificial lamb, and Gray would be the one who exercised the knife, sliced the blade through the sinews of her career.

"Effectively you're offering me a step up the ladder at a colleague's expense."

Carslake grimaced. "Not quite how I'd put it, Sol. Think about it another way. You've more than paid your dues. You should be an inspector already. You deserve this. Any promotion would be on merit."

"I'm not a back stabber."

"I never said you were!"

"It's what you want me to do though, Jeff."

"No, no. Simply to facilitate the initial step. Have a think about it, okay? Take your time, I need to see the Usher investigation through and satisfactorily closed before anything meaningful can happen anyway." Carslake checked his watch. "Ouch, look at the time. I'd better get back. And you seem about ready to fall asleep. You're shattered, go home and get some rest. In fact, take a few days off." Carslake stood up. "And

Sol, not a word to anyone about Hamson's demise. This is entirely between us."

Nine

Then
    "Get dressed," said the friend, the one he'd called on.
    "What's the point?" he shrugged. "She's dead. I killed her. I'm finished."
    "That's not happening. If you go down, I do too." The friend scooped the killer's trousers off the floor and threw them at his feet. "Sort yourself out." The friend turned away, leaving him alone.
    He rose to his feet and slowly pulled his clothes on, keeping his back to Valerie. By the time he was buttoning his shirt the friend was back, carrying a vacuum cleaner, a cloth and several plastic carrier bags in his gloved hands. The friend handed the cloth to him and a pair of gloves.
    "Put those on then wipe anything you might have touched. If they find your fingerprints all over the place they'll wonder why. Vacuum the floor then put the hoover contents into a bag."
    "I know what to do."
    "If that were true, we wouldn't be standing here now."
    "Sorry."
    "There's no time for recrimination. Get on with it. At least you had the good sense to use a condom. Which reminds me, you'll have to clean her too."
    "Why?"

"God, think about it, man! Pubes. They get everywhere. The vacuum hose should do it."

"Really?"

The friend grabbed him by the shirt, pulled him close. He could hear the rasp in his friend's throat as he fought for control. "I'm very close to walking out and leaving you with this. Pull yourself together."

He looked down at his feet. "Sorry."

The friend let go. "Did you go anywhere else in the house? Do anything else?"

"We had a cup of coffee in the kitchen."

"That's it? Think! We haven't got long."

"Yes, that's it."

"Right, you get this cleared up, the dishwasher can deal with the cups. We need to get out of here as soon as possible."

The friend left the room while he switched the vacuum on and began sucking up the evidence of his presence, the last remnants of the affair.

Ten

N^{ow} The restaurant was at the bottom of Harbour Street, a narrow thoroughfare which led down to the Broadstairs sea front and jetty. Across the road, a tired amusement arcade failed to lure clientele with its flashing lights, half of them burnt out. Next door to that, a tiny cinema in a flint and brick building claimed its fame of being among the smallest such joints in the country. A portcullis arch spanned the road joining the restaurant to the sailing club, attesting to Broadstairs' more violent past.

The restaurant was a far more modern expanse of windows, designed so the diners could take in the sea view. But this also meant pedestrians could observe what the diners were eating.

Usher pushed open the door. The interior was dark lacquered flooring and mismatched tables, white-painted brick walls organised into three tiers which dropped down over successive floors, each with its own large Edison light chandelier, aligned with the angle of the descending road outside. A mishmash of different sized and shaped mirrors were affixed to the far walls. A bar area stretched across the width of the upper tier. It was busy, a hubbub of chatter, relaxed patrons enjoying the atmosphere.

"Hello, sir," said a greeter. She wore black trousers and a polo shirt with the restaurant's logo sewn in, complete with a maroon apron tied around her waist. A badge revealed her name. *Jenny.* She was young, fresh-faced, freckles on her cheeks. Her hair was tied into a fishbone plait. She smiled, revealing a gap between her front teeth. "Would you like to dine with us today?"

"Absolutely," said Usher.

"A table for how many?"

"Two." Usher looked up at the CCTV lens above and behind the bar. "Mr McGavin is expecting me."

"That's wonderful. We have a table with an excellent sea view reserved for you both. I hope that's all right?"

"Lead on."

Jenny took two menus from the bar area before heading down the stairs. Usher followed. On the way Jenny touched one of her colleagues on her arm, nodded at her. The table was small and packed tightly into a corner on the lowest level. The chair was rickety and Usher felt hemmed in, the diners practically seated on top of each other. But Jenny was right; the view out across the beach and rippling sea was excellent.

Jenny placed a menu in front of Usher and said, "Your waitress today is Naomi." It was the same woman Jenny had tapped. "If you need anything don't hesitate to ask. Mr McGavin will be with you shortly." Jenny withdrew.

"Good afternoon, sir," said Naomi. She was older than Jenny, a tinge of grey in her clipped-back brown hair. She had a round face and dark skin. She put a basket with several types of white and brown bread and a carafe of water dappled with condensation in front of him.

"Specials of the day are mussels to start and locally caught skate as the main course." Naomi pointed to them on the menu. Usher glanced at the prices. Food cost a lot more these days. She pulled a pad from a pocket in the apron and a pen from her shirt. "Would you like to order a drink or wait until Mr McGavin arrives?"

"How about a bottle of wine? It's been a while since I last drank, so could you suggest something? Nothing cheap, of course."

Naomi nodded. "Certainly. Our wine waiter is very knowledgeable."

"Then I trust his judgement."

Naomi smiled and headed for the bar. Usher grabbed a piece of bread from the basket and popped it into his mouth. He'd only eaten prison food for the last decade and a half and wasn't sure what to make of the bread's floral flavour. A thick layer of butter helped. Naomi returned and angled a bottle of Malbec so he could read the label. "Is this acceptable?"

"Excellent choice." Usher had no idea if it was or wasn't.

Naomi popped the cork and poured a small amount into a glass. "Do you want to taste it?"

"No, I'm sure it's great. Keep going. I'll say when." After fifteen years of no alcohol, this was going to be interesting. She'd filled the glass almost to the lip by the time Usher stopped her.

"You'll have a hangover tomorrow," said McGavin who was standing behind Naomi. She moved to let him past. McGavin unbuttoned his suit jacket as he sat. "Thanks, Naomi. Have you ordered, Duncan?"

"Not yet."

"Can I make a suggestion?"

"Go ahead."

McGavin pointed at the menu before Naomi delivered the orders to the kitchen.

"We'll be treated as a priority," McGavin said, as he leaned in towards Usher.

"I never saw you as a restaurateur, Frank."

"Us, Duncan. This is your business more than mine. And mid-range dining is the rage these days. People pay good money for honest, locally sourced food." McGavin picked up the Malbec, peered at the label. "You've got good taste."

"Apparently we have a superb wine waiter." Usher took a tentative sip. The berry flavours flooded his mouth. He savoured them momentarily before taking a second, deeper draw. McGavin smiled.

"I'll congratulate her later."

"I've missed that. You'll join me, of course?"

"I have a rule. No alcohol when I'm working." McGavin laughed when he saw the expression on Usher's face. "Though today is an exception." McGavin got himself a glass and poured. He clinked glasses with Usher. "Great to see you. It's been a while."

"Cheers." Usher looked McGavin over, noted the expensive suit, the crisply ironed white shirt, the gold cufflinks. "You've put on weight." McGavin appeared successful, a man who'd achieved much for somebody only recently into their forties.

"You're thinner."

"Jail time." Usher knew it had aged him, he looked much older than McGavin though there was only a decade between them.

The waitress brought two dishes over to the table.

"Scallops," said McGavin. "Fresh off the boat this morning in Ramsgate. As I said, we use as many local ingredients as possible."

Usher picked up a fork, poked around in the upturned scallop shell.

"There aren't any extra ingredients."

"Old habits die hard." Usher ladled a chunk into his mouth.

"How is it?"

"All right," admitted Usher, his mouth half full. "I've had worse." He smiled. It was excellent, to be fair. The scallop had a soft, melting texture which barely resisted his teeth. A scoop of lightly minted mushy peas and a shard of well-done, almost burnt, streaky bacon added unusual contrasting flavours.

"I guess you'll be wanting to take the reins back?" McGavin picked at a scallop himself.

"Does that bother you, Frank?"

"Why would it?"

"Be straight with me."

McGavin sighed, sipped some more wine. "All right, I'll hold my hands up. I'm used to being the boss after all this time, but a deal is a deal. I said I'd look after the business until you got out."

"And here I am."

"Yes."

Naomi arrived back at the table. "May I clear your plates?"

"Thank you," said McGavin.

"I've an alternative proposal," said Usher once Naomi had gone. He'd been thinking about this for a while. McGavin waited, twirling his glass. "How about you continue to run the day-to-day operations and I sit in the background?"

McGavin thought about it briefly. "Like Managing Director and Chairman?"

"Exactly like that. The older, wiser man delegates and reaps the rewards from the harder working upstart."

McGavin laughed. "I can live with that."

"Good." Usher held his hand out for McGavin to shake.

"Can I do anything to help? Money, for example? There's a car at your disposal, of course and Dean to drive you."

"I'm okay for cash, though I could do with somewhere to stay."

"I thought you might." McGavin laid a set of keys on the table. There's a flat just above Beaches, around the corner."

"Where?"

"Sorry, Beaches is a café on Albion Street. Turn left at the top, you can't miss it."

Usher scooped up the keys and pocketed them. "Thanks."

"No need." McGavin held up his hands, palms out. "Given you did a stretch for Dean and me, it's the least we can do."

The waitress delivered the main course. A rib-eye steak, rare, the blood seeping out of the meat. A small stack of chips, organised in a Jenga-style block, a few salad leaves and some peas in a small glass bowl. There was a white jug with peppercorn sauce too.

"How's that?" asked McGavin.

Usher raised his eyebrows at the neatly arranged meal, surprised at how little there appeared to be on the plate. "I guess this place makes good profits?"

"Decent enough, yes."

McGavin picked up his knife and fork and asked, "What's next?"

"Figuring out which of the bastards set me up." Usher devoured the steak, surprised at suddenly how hungry he was, shoving a piece of meat into his mouth as he was swallowing the previous chunk.

"Who do you think it was?"

The who – Copeland, Carslake or Gray. "Could be any of them," shrugged Usher. "Or all of them."

"Then?"

"Kill them."

"We haven't got the garage anymore."

Where they used to deal with the inconveniences. "Doesn't matter. I'll find a way."

"You always did, Duncan."

"Have you seen my girls recently?"

"I keep an eye on them." Neither lived on Thanet now. "They're both doing well. Do you want to see them?"

"Once this is over."

"Dessert?" asked McGavin when Usher pushed his plate away.

"Couldn't eat another thing."

"Anytime you want, come in. I'll ensure all the staff knows who you are. They'll take good care of you. You are the boss, after all."

"Thanks."

Usher and McGavin stood. They shook hands once more. Usher nodded to Jenny as he left the restaurant and got a broad grin in response. He turned right and climbed up Harbour Street. At the junction with Albion Street, where three pubs faced each other, he avoided temptation and crossed the road to a car park. Telfer, his driver, was leaning against the car, located in a disabled spot, picking at his finger nails with a pen knife.

"How did it go?" asked Telfer as he straightened and slid the blade closed.

"About as well as you'd expect."

Telfer opened the door for Usher. "Where now?"

"Gray."

Eleven

Then

"Duncan fucking Usher, eh? What a breakthrough this could be!" said Copeland. He stared at Valerie's body.

"A dead woman is hardly what I'd call a breakthrough," snapped Carslake.

"All right, DS Carslake, remember who you're talking to."

"I just think we should be specific, sir. At the moment it appears to be a murder suicide with a suspect in custody who isn't Usher. Plus Usher's girls are missing."

"Attempted suicide, Jeff. And you know what I mean. I'd bet my left bollock Usher is involved. He has to be."

Copeland was a career-first type of detective. He'd moved over from Herefordshire nearly eighteen months ago and was determined to stamp an impression of his large boot on the area. Arresting Usher and making a charge stick, a feat none of his predecessors had managed, would make that print indelibly deep and permanent. Copeland had a style about him which neither Gray nor Carslake were keen on and there was hardly a basis for Copeland's current judgement. But Copeland had been the one who'd given Gray his chance to work in CID. And he was the boss, so Gray kept quiet.

"DI Copeland, I'd really like to get back to work," said Brazier.

"I'm not stopping you."

"Please can you leave the room, space is rather tight."

"Your wish is my command." Copeland led his officers onto the landing. Shaking his head, Copeland said loud enough to be heard by Brazier and his team, "Bloody SOCO, they should know they're not the brains of this outfit. Just the tools, literally."

Brazier stiffened, but said nothing, choosing to ignore the jibe.

"Yes, sir," said Carslake. Gray knew he didn't agree with Copeland, but like Brazier, Carslake had learned when to comply. Which was most of the time. Carslake possessed this innate ability to play the political game, to say the pleasing words, to take the right action – something he kept coaching Gray on. Gray was trying his best to emulate his DS, but it didn't come easily.

"Summarise the situation for me, Jeff," said Copeland. Carslake did so. When he'd finished, Copeland was silent for a few moments, thinking. "We're missing a lot of data here," he said. "The woman's bedroom is clearly the locus. I want any fingerprints, hair samples, whatever, analysed in double quick time. I don't care about the cost. They're top priority. Understand?"

"Yes, sir."

"The knife; is it from the house or brought in from the outside?"

"Impossible to say at this stage," Carslake said. "There's a drawer full of utensils of various brands."

"No convenient block of wood with one blade obviously missing?"

"Unfortunately not."

"There never is."

"What about the bloke you found beside the woman's body?"

"Word from the hospital is he's undergoing an operation. He'd lost a lot of blood. Much longer and he might not have been alive."

"I want to talk to him as soon as he's conscious. Have uniform stationed by his bed."

"Already organised, sir, along with a door-to-door and we're contacting next of kin."

"Good, you're learning. Might make a half-decent copper out of you at some point if you carry on like this."

"I appreciate it, sir."

Copeland's self-importance was a characteristic Carslake had complained to Gray about over a beer several times. Wisely, Carslake bit his tongue. Copeland's approach was send only.

"Don't knock it, Jeff. The ability to study your betters is a useful trait in rising up the ranks. Everybody needs a helping hand at one time or another." Copeland paused to ensure the message had got through to Carslake. "What about his identity?"

"Nothing definitive but we were discussing this as you arrived, sir." Carslake held up the phone. "Just the one number stored in the memory. Says 'home'."

"Has anybody called it yet?"

"We were about to."

"What's the number? I'll do that now?"

Carslake read out the detail of the number and Copeland tapped it into his own phone. He pressed the green key, then the button for the speaker and waited. The call connected and was answered on the first ring.

"Hello?" A woman's voice, urgent.

"This is Detective Inspector Copeland, who am I speaking to?"

"Molly Mundby, do you have news about Craig? My son, he's missing. I called in a report earlier. He has some mental health issues."

"Can you describe him please?"

Molly did so, it matched the man they'd found beside Valerie."

"I'm afraid to say your son has been involved in an incident."

Molly cut across Copeland. "What incident? Is he all right? Where is he?"

"Craig has been taken to hospital."

"I'm going there now." Molly cut the call.

"We'll deal with that later," said Copeland, as he hit the "end" button and slid the phone into his pocket. "Show me the rest."

Gray walked Carslake and Copeland around the house, starting with the lounge. Gray pulled at the handle of one of the large windows. He stepped into a decent-sized garden which would probably have a sea view on the horizon during the day.

The garden was mostly lawn with mature shrubs and border plants around the extremities. A path wound its way across the centre, like stepping stones across a green lake. A tall tree hung over one corner, the leaves rustling gently. Gray had no idea what any one of the plants was called. He'd never possessed green fingers. Opposite the tree was a shed, also locked.

"Not easy to get around the back of the property," said Gray, pointing at high, wooden fences which ran the perimeter.

"There's a side gate too. A narrow path on the right-hand side of the house," said Carslake, "but the gate's locked and at the moment we can't find the key."

"Hell of a lot of security for such a quiet area," said Copeland. "Electric gates, an alarm, and a camera."

"That's what we thought."

"Talk to the company, see when it was all put in and access the camera footage."

"I'll do that," said Gray. There was a name on the alarm box, Raptor Security, and a local phone number. Gray noted it down. He caught movement in the corner of his eye. Fowler at the windows. "Sir." Gray nodded at Fowler.

Copeland turned, said, "What is it, lad?"

"Sorry to interrupt sir," he said. "Next of kin has turned up a name, Eva Franklin. She's Valerie Usher's mother."

"And?"

"The daughters are with her."

"That's a relief," said Carslake.

"What's her address?"

Fowler handed over a piece of paper which Copeland folded into his pocket without even glancing at it. "She'll have to wait, though. Usher first."

Twelve

N^{ow} Gray leaned against the front door of his flat to close it and dropped his bag on the floor. He stayed where he was for a few moments, head hung low. He rubbed his eyes. They felt gritty and sore. When he took his hand away from his face it shook.

Although he felt worst immediately following radiotherapy, the after-effects stayed with him for weeks. He was permanently short of energy and drive. The pretence he had to maintain made it worse, giving the appearance of normality when all he wanted to do was lie in bed. He'd picked up his post from the box downstairs; one of the envelopes had a frank from the local hospital. It would be about his next appointment. Gray couldn't face that right now.

"You look ancient, Sol. The last fifteen years haven't been kind to you."

Gray started with surprise. Sitting cross-legged on his sofa was Duncan Usher, a mug on one knee. Gray had been so drained he hadn't even noticed his presence. "How the hell did you get in?"

"Old dog, old tricks, my friend."

"Get out."

Usher raised the mug. "I've already made myself at home. Why would I leave?"

"Where's Telfer?"

"With the car. If you look down onto the pavement you'll see him." Usher picked up a pawn from the coffee table. Gray had a game in progress. "I didn't fancy you for a chess geek."

"So?"

Usher put the piece back down, but not in the right place. "Make yourself a drink and join me, I've something you'll want to hear." Usher stood up, crossed to the large glass doors which led onto the balcony where Gray regularly sat, whatever the weather, and slid one open. Outside were a table and an accompanying chair.

Gray opened the front door for Usher to leave through. "I severely doubt I'd be interested in anything you had to say."

"It's about Tom."

Gray froze. It was the last thing he'd have expected Usher to say. "What about him?"

Usher shook his head. "Make a coffee first. You need an injection of energy. Kettle's not long boiled." Usher turned away from Gray and bent over the balcony, resting his arms on the railings.

His mind whirling, Gray made himself a coffee. While he waited for the grounds to steep he tried to think what Usher would want. But he couldn't decide – whatever it was, he knew it wouldn't be good and there was no point second guessing a man like Usher. He went out onto the balcony.

"Great view," said Usher, straightening. He'd brought the chess set out with him, reset the pieces to their start positions. "I thought we could have a game."

Up close Gray could see other, more subtle changes in Usher that hadn't been clear from the television interview. He'd clearly kept himself fit in the gym; he was lithe and moved with an evident strength. But there was a twist to his expression that wasn't there in the past. The weight of prison time on his shoulders. Usher had always been a good-looking man, armed with charm and wit. It appeared to have been replaced with a degree of bitterness and bile.

"Not interested," said Gray.

"You look knackered," said Usher, "have the chair."

"I'm fine. What are you playing at?"

Usher opened his hands in an appeal. "Besides chess, I've no idea what you mean, Sol."

"Don't use my first name. We're not friends and we never have been. In fact, I don't think you've ever had a friend in your life besides Telfer and McGavin."

"Now you're just being cruel."

"I don't care what you think, Usher. What do you want?"

"Isn't it obvious? The same as you."

"There's nothing about us that overlaps."

"Oh yes, there is. We've both lost our family and never recovered."

"You wrecked that yourself. Somebody else destroyed mine."

"No, Sol. Nothing happens by accident. Somebody destroyed both of us. I've a suspicion it was one and the same person."

"I worked on your case, I know what happened."

"Do you? If that's true, why am I out, and why are you the one being investigated now?"

"What the hell are you talking about? I'm a cop; you're a newly released criminal."

Usher simply smiled. "We can help each other."

"I don't need your help."

"But I want yours."

"What could I possibly be interested in doing for you?"

"Let's take the how first. I've been away for a long time and I'll not be wasting any more. I want justice, and you can speed the whole process up for me. Being on the inside, feeding me information. The why is because by doing so it would put me forever in your debt. I always pay what I owe."

"Go through the normal channels. I'm sure your lawyer can give suitable advice."

"Don't worry, he's pressing hard. But he's on the outside, so to speak. As I said, it would be optimum to have somebody within."

"I'm not breaking the law for you."

Usher shook his head in mock disappointment. "Nobody's incorruptible, Gray. We all have a weakness. Yours is Tom."

"Don't say his name."

"Or what? You'll fight me? You can barely lift your arm, old man. What is it? Prostate? Pretty common in men of our age, and I've seen enough of it over the years."

"None of your business."

"I heard you were up in Edinburgh, making up for lost time."

Gray didn't answer, surprised Usher knew so much about him. He could have made a lucky guess about the cancer, but Edinburgh? Somebody must have told him that and not many people knew where Gray had been in recent days.

"Hasn't it been on your mind, Sol? That time's slipping away? That you may never see Tom before you go?"

"I'll find him."

"Maybe not fast enough though, before your illness eats you from the inside out. I can give him to you."

"Utter bullshit."

"Is it? Wouldn't you grasp any chance to finally know?" Usher held up his hands, pushing his palms theatrically at Gray. "It's okay, you don't need to say, I know the answer because we're the same."

"We're nothing alike, Usher."

"I'd give anything, anything to get my girls back. I haven't seen them for fifteen years. They're grown up and Elodie's married. I didn't get the chance to walk her down the aisle or give a speech at the wedding. I'm a grandparent, and I don't even know the child's name. Every day I think about them. If the person who set me up was here, right now..." Usher held his mug out over the drop and opened his fingers. A few seconds later there was the smash of breaking china. "I think you would too, Sol. Am I right?"

Gray bit down on his own admission, not willing to share anything with Usher. "How can I trust you?"

Usher sat down, his back to Gray. "You shouldn't." Usher began to move the chess pieces, playing both black and white. A couple of pawns, a castle and then a bishop. "We don't need to be on opposing sides, Sol, facing off against each other. Help me, I help you. A straightforward business transaction. Are you with me?"

Gray wanted to say yes, but equally he was wary. Getting in bed with the other side of the law...

He said, "I don't know."

"You have my word that I'll get Tom back to you."

"I need time to think."

"Fair enough. In the interim take a look at Copeland. I'll be in touch."

AFTER USHER LEFT, GRAY remained on the balcony, listening to the rush of the waves beneath him. Usually they were a calming harmonic, but not right now. Too much was going through his mind.

Gray was conflicted. He believed Usher when he talked about his family and wanting justice. But Usher's methods were different to Gray's. And Tom. *He was still out there, somewhere.* But could he trust Usher? Most of him said no.

However, Gray had ignored that part of his conscience for too many years to start now. He'd sailed close to the wind before, working with Marcus Pennance and his group of paedophile hunters. Taking home confidential case notes, undertaking his own investigation. He'd nearly been fired over it. Only Carslake had kept him in a job. Gray had learned over the years the wider the circle of people involved, the greater the risk of being found out. Who else could he trust?

He'd lost all confidence in Carslake. Gray's friendship with Hamson was on the rocks. That meant only two people. Mike Fowler was one, but for all his faults, at least he stuck to the rules when it came to police work. Fowler's personal life was another matter. His affair with Hamson, for example. Fowler had fallen out publicly with Gray, assuming Gray had slept with Fowler's wife but eventually Fowler had admitted he was wrong and they'd become friends again. However, for now he'd have to keep Fowler in reserve and only approach him if absolutely necessary.

Which left Pennance. Gray went back inside, closed the door, picked up his mobile and scrolled through the numbers.

"Sol," said Pennance when he answered. "It's been a while."

"I need a favour."

"Still getting straight to the point as usual, then?"

"Sorry, lots on my mind."

"Tell me something I don't know. What do you need?"

"Have you heard of Eric Smits? He's a senior investigator with the IPCC."

"The name's not familiar. Do you want me to look into him?"

"If it's not a problem."

"With you, Sol, it's always a problem. But yes, I'll check him out."

"Thanks."

"How have you managed to get yourself tangled up with the IPCC?"

"It's Usher."

"I saw that on the news. I wondered if it involved you. I should have known. If there's trouble at hand you're always involved."

"Smits is arriving tomorrow. Along with an Emily Wyatt."

"Now she's a name I recognise. She's with CEOP."

CEOP. *Child Exploitation and Online Protection.* They were a wing of the IPCC. Gray wondered what precisely that meant.

"Have you been involved with an IPCC investigation before, Sol?"

"No."

"I suggest you read up on the procedure."

"It'll be dull and boring, they always are."

"You're not far wrong."

"I can tell you now, I won't have the patience."

Pennance sighed. "Do you want a quick summary?"

"Thanks. If I read something like that through in entirety I'll end up chucking myself off the balcony." Gray remembered Usher's mug.

"Fundamentally, Sol, the purpose of an investigation is to establish the facts behind a complaint."

"Obviously."

"Okay, if you know everything already I won't bother wasting any more of your time."

"Okay, okay. I'll shut up."

"First sensible comment you've made all night. The investigator's role is to determine the facts of the case. If at any time it appears to the investigator a person may have committed a criminal offence or behaved in a manner justifying disciplinary proceedings, then the investigator must place the investigation under special requirements." Pennance sounded just like a document, but Gray held his tongue.

Pennance continued, "Severity assessments must be made ASAP on the basis of what would happen if the conduct was proved. Misconduct is a breach of standards of professional behaviour. Gross misconduct is a breach so serious that dismissal would be justified.

"When the investigator has completed a severity assessment a written notice must go to the subject unless it might prejudice the investigation. I'd strongly suggest that if either of the investigators wants to meet, then you have someone you can trust beside you as a witness."

"That would have to be Fowler."

"Was he involved in the original investigation?"

"On the periphery. He was in uniform and manned the perimeter cordon at the murder scene."

"You might have a problem there. Fowler will probably be considered to have a bias. Anybody else you could ask?"

"What about you?"

Pennance laughed. "Just get whoever you choose to keep copious notes."

"Okay."

"An interviewee isn't entitled to see all evidence."

"So they could have stuff on me and I'd never know?"

"Theoretically, yes. Smits' only obligation is to keep the complainant informed of progress at least every 28 days. Lastly, you can either be a witness or a subject of the investigation. Smits will have to tell you which it is, in writing. If it's a witness, you'll just be looked upon to give evidence. If you're a subject—"

"I'm in the shit."

"Pretty much. Then it's up to Smits to carry out a severity assessment. Are your actions misconduct or gross misconduct? Do you get a warning or dismissal? They could even decide there's a criminal case to answer."

"I can't see that happening."

"Hopefully not." Pennance didn't sound convinced. "So, is that it? Have I got off lightly for once? Just a short speech?"

"Unfortunately not."

Pennance sighed. "Go on."

"I need access to the original Usher case files."

"You don't make things easy for me, Sol."

"Can you do it or not, Marcus?"

"I'll get the details. And I won't ask why."

"Don't take any risks on my behalf."

Pennance laughed. "Do you know how ridiculous that sounds?" Gray couldn't bring himself to join in. "It'll be tomorrow."

"Thanks, I appreciate it."

Pennance said goodbye and cut the call. Gray picked up his case from the hall where he'd left it and took it into the bedroom to unpack. He unzipped the case, lifting out the vanity bag containing his medication. He went to the bathroom, tipped out a couple of the pills and swallowed them with a glass of water before putting the bottles away in the cabinet above the sink. He felt a headache coming on, but decided against some paracetamol. He had enough drugs in his body.

After unpacking his clothes, Gray collected his mug from the balcony and went into the kitchen. On the side, was the letter from the hospital. He picked it up, tore along the top of the envelope and pulled out a single sheet of paper. He was right. An appointment for further treatment. At the worst possible time, he'd be laid low again. Gray put the letter down. He'd deal with it later.

Gray's phone rang. It was Pennance again. "I just spoke to some friends. Smits is ex-Serious Organised Crime Agency. Before SOCA merged with the National Crime Agency it wasn't unusual for the IPCC to use their staff. Smits shifted over to the IPCC with the merger. His presence might mean something or nothing, but don't expect an easy ride from him. I reckon this investigation will be classified as a DSI matter – death or serious injury – or maybe corruption."

"I can't believe it'll go that far."

"Usher was imprisoned for fifteen years for a crime it seems he didn't commit. You know what senior management is like. We live in a world where blame has to be apportioned and 'lessons learned.'" Gray clearly heard Pennance's emphasis down the line. "And all of this in public view."

"Copeland was SIO. It's him they'll want."

"I hope you're right."

"Thanks for the information, it's a big help."

"Remember, record everything and say as little as possible."

"I know the drill."

"You'd be surprised how many cops forget that when they're on the other side of the table."

Gray said goodbye and disconnected. He was even more puzzled than before he spoke to Pennance. Wyatt from child protection and Smits with a background in corruption.

What the hell did it all mean?

Thirteen

T**hen** Gray's headlights lit up the twin towers of Kingsgate Castle. He parked beside the gate, inset within high flint-encased walls, beneath crenellated battlements.

"All the years I've lived in Thanet, and I've never been inside the castle," said Gray.

"Because it's exclusive," said Carslake, "not for the likes of us."

The place had been built in the late 18th century for Lord Holland – a huge, meandering construction assembled as a faux fort simply for the lord's horses and associated staff. Holland's larger house was long gone. A decade or so ago the castle had been converted into thirty-one apartments, one of which was owned by Duncan Usher. The building sat on the clifftop above Joss Bay, just along from the North Foreland, location of the last manned lighthouse in the UK and the most exclusive area on the island.

"We're not here for a nostalgia tour," said Copeland as he got out. He strode through the portcullis gate, not pausing for his men. Gray, after locking the car, followed.

Usher was awaiting them in the cobbled courtyard. He was a powerful man in all senses of the word. Heavily built without being fat, large hands, black hair shaved in a buzz cut close to the skull. He had a presence. When he was in the room you knew it. But he wasn't ostentatious; for all that he was probably the wealthiest man on the island. Usher preferred to keep his operations and the results under wraps.

"Good evening, officers," said Usher, offering his hand, which Gray then Carslake shook. Copeland declined, eliciting a smile from Usher. He led them to an open doorway in the far wall from which light spilled. Inside were stone steps spiralling aloft. One floor up was the entrance to Usher's residence. Gray entered a hallway, his feet sinking into deep carpet.

Usher closed the large wooden door, dark with age, behind Gray. "Do you gentlemen want anything to drink?" he asked.

"We're fine," said Copeland.

"In that case, let's talk in the lounge. Second door on your left."

Once through a similarly heavy wooden door studded with iron, arched in the shape of the stone surround, it was obvious by the curved shape of the room that Usher's apartment was located in one of the towers.

"Nice view," said Copeland. Windows opened out onto the sea, nothing in front to interrupt the near one-hundred-and-eighty-degree vista.

"I like it," said Usher. He crossed the room to a low, long cupboard constructed from a similarly dark wood, mahogany maybe, and lifted a bottle up. "Can I call you Terry?"

"No."

Usher grinned, like this was all some game to him. "Are you sure you won't join me?"

"Thanks, but we're on duty."

"Of course."

Usher poured himself a drink into a brandy snifter before sitting in one of the leather armchairs. He crossed one leg over the other. Copeland took a seat directly opposite, leaving the sofa to Gray and Carslake. The furnishings were a clash of old and new. Along with the armchairs, a matching sofa was arranged around a glass-topped table. The backdrop was the curved walls of the tower, lined with paper covered in heraldic motifs. Then there were large pieces of modern art. A bronze sculpture in a seemingly random shape only the artist would understand.

Getting straight to the point, Copeland asked, "What were your movements earlier this evening, between 7 p.m. and 9 p.m.?"

"I was here."

Gray made a note in his book.

"What time did you arrive?"

"Around six, I'd say."

"Any witnesses to your movements?"

"I live alone, Inspector."

"So that's a no?"

"Correct."

Carslake stood. "Where's the bathroom?"

"I'll show you." Usher made to get up.

"No need," said Copeland. "He's a big boy and can find his own way."

"Upstairs one more flight, straight ahead of you."

"Thanks."

Usher frowned as Carslake left the room.

"What about your driver – Telfer?"

"Dean is more confidante than lackey. And I drove myself. Earlier in the day, I was visiting my children. I don't need to drag Dean along to that."

"At your ex-wife's address?"

"She's not my ex-wife." Usher paused. "Wasn't," he corrected. He sank half the brandy. "I can't believe she's dead."

"I CAN'T BELIEVE SHE'S dead." He was sat on the end of the bed.

"What's done is done," said his friend from the doorway. "Sooner you get your head around it, the better chance we've got of surviving your monumental balls up."

He dipped his head.

"And you can stop that too."

"What?"

"Feeling sorry for yourself. You have to take this memory, put it in a box, bury it deep, and throw away the key. You can beg for mercy when you're dead. The police are going to be here soon, picking this place over. You can't afford to show any weakness now."

"Okay." He nodded. He knew his friend was right. This was what he needed right now; a firm hand, smacking him back to the present. It was why he'd made the call.

"Have you vacuumed up?" asked the friend.

"Yes."

"Wiped up?"

"Yes."

"Every surface?"

"Yes, for Christ's sake! I'm not stupid."

The look his buddy gave him revealed exactly what he thought. *You idiot.* "You've missed one thing."

"What?"

"You're sitting on it."

He stood, stared at the indentation where his backside had just been.

"The sheet," said the friend. "You'll be all over it. Give me a hand to take it off."

Working together, either side of the bed, the pair unhitched the corners of the bedsheet from the mattress before the friend pulled it steadily from beneath Valerie like a slow motion magic trick. When the sheet was free, the friend balled it up roughly then threw it at him.

"Put that inside a carrier bag," said the friend. He ran his eyes over the room. "I think we're done here. Let's go."

It was when they got outside that the friend's careful plan began to unravel. He stopped in the doorway, holding him back.

"Who's that?" The friend pointed to a figure across the road.

He groaned. "He knows me."

"Then he needs sorting out."

"YOU WERE SEPARATED though?" asked Copeland.

"Actually, we were in the process of rebuilding our relationship," said Usher. He smiled ruefully. "We'd maintained an outwardly friendly relationship throughout, for the sake of the girls."

"Why did she leave?"

"Because she didn't like the life I led. To be a successful businessman has a consequential impact on your friends and family. Sacrifices have to be made. It was tough on Lotty and Elodie."

"What changed?"

"I recently told her I was retiring, that it was time to do something new. That's what brought us back together."

"This new life, was it inside or outside the criminal fraternity, Mr Usher?"

Usher gave a small, ironic laugh. "It doesn't matter now either way."

"No, I suppose not. Funny how things work out."

"If you say so, Inspector."

"How long had you been apart?"

"About a year. Enough for us both to realise we were better as a pair, for the girls."

"I assume your relationship was close?"

"Not anymore, but I was hoping we'd be drawn to each other by spending more time in each other's company and focusing on the children."

"Falling in love all over again?"

"If you like."

"How was Mrs Usher when you last saw her?"

"Happier than normal."

Copeland frowned. "What does that mean?"

Usher finished his brandy, stood, crossed to the cupboard and poured himself another. He stared into the contents while he swirled. "She's hard to describe, Inspector."

"Try, please."

Usher sipped at the brandy. "Val was often unpredictable."

"In what way?"

"She liked spur-of-the-moment decisions."

"Like you and her getting back together?"

"That was a long time coming, certainly not a knee-jerk re-action." Usher sat back down. "She could be maddening. Never happy, no matter how much I gave her; striving for more, even though she didn't need it. I amply provided." Usher spread his arms, meaning the obvious wealth of the apartment. "Though recently she seemed to have calmed down, accepted where she was, who she was, maybe."

"Do you know why?"

"I thought because of us being a couple again."

"You're not so sure now?"

"After this, I don't know what to think."

"When did you arrive at your wife's?"

"I got there for lunch. We ate leisurely; I went into the gar-den with the girls for a bit, took them to the park at the end of the road and left before they all had dinner."

"And the girls were still there then?"

"Yes."

"Do you know Craig Mundby?"

"He's one of the gardeners. Seems like a good kid. What's he got to do with anything?"

"At this stage, I don't know. I'm just asking questions."

The door opened. Usher swivelled his head towards Carslake as he entered the room. "You took your time. Do I need to fumigate the bathroom?"

"I took a call. I didn't want to disturb you all."

"I think we're done here for now anyway," said Copeland. "Thanks for your time Mr Usher."

"Just find her killer." Usher stood. "I'll show you out."

Fourteen

N^ow Gray arrived late for the start of his shift. He'd had a restless night, overslept, hurriedly got dressed, only to be stuck in the rush-hour traffic. He draped his jacket over the back of his chair, turned on the PC, and went to make a coffee in the makeshift tea room that was shoved into a corner of the office.

"Anyone else want one?" shouted Gray with the kettle poised beneath the tap. No takers except Fowler who stood up and crossed over while the water cascaded into the kettle. Gray flicked the switch and pulled two mugs and a French press from a cupboard, then put them onto the chipped formica work surface.

"They've been looking for you," said Fowler in a low voice. "The two of them from IPCC, Smits and Wyatt. Sounds like an American cowboy show."

"What are they like?"

"She's ice cold, he's a puffer fish."

Gray frowned, puzzled by Fowler's description.

"You'll see," said Fowler. "Anyway, I need your help with something."

"Sure." The kettle boiling, Gray let it rest while he measured out grinds into the cafetière.

"I want to file a complaint about Yvonne breaking my helicopter yesterday."

Gray paused his coffee-making process. "Seriously?"

"Of course."

"You've been irritating everybody with that thing for ages." The kettle clicked off.

"Ironic really because Yvonne bought it for me." So Hamson was the bloody idiot. Gray poured some water onto the coffee. "Will you, though?"

"No, Mike."

"Why?"

"Isn't it obvious? She's our boss and relationships are tough enough as it is."

"That's what everybody else has said."

"Then take that as a hint and drop it."

"You're a lot of help." The sarcasm was obvious in Fowler's tone. "Thanks, mate."

Gray grabbed Fowler's forearm. "Seriously, Mike there's times when it's best to turn around and walk."

"And how often have you done that?" Fowler pushed Gray's hand off.

"I'll bring your coffee over in a minute when it's brewed."

An unfamiliar face entered the Detectives' Office. He was tall, possessed bulbous features and a bald skull, except for a stripe of greying hair along one side of his head. Gray wondered why he didn't shave everything off. This must be Smits, given Fowler's earlier aquatic comment. Smits scanned the room, spotted Gray, and made his way over. Fowler drifted back to his desk, facing away from Gray and Smits.

"Ah, Sergeant Gray? I'm Eric Smits." Smits' grip was dry and firm. "I wondered if you might have ten minutes for me? Nothing serious." Smits smiled.

"Do you mind if I do something first?"

"Feel free. We're not here to interfere in the day-to-day operation of Thanet CID."

"That's good to know."

"I'd heard you like your coffee." Smits nodded at Gray's mug.

"Oh? Been checking up on me?"

"No need, you're quite the character around here. It seems everybody has a word to say about you." Gray didn't rise to the obvious bait. "Anyway, we've taken an office upstairs next to DCI Carslake. I'm sure you'll find us. When you're ready, Sergeant."

"Sure."

Smits turned and left. Gray realised the whole office was watching him. He poured his coffee and carried one over to Fowler, who complained about the lack of sugar. For the moment Smits needed to wait.

Gray left his mug on his desk and headed to Hamson. "Ma'am," he said, "can I have a word?"

"I'm in the middle of writing a report for the DCI, Sergeant." Hamson kept her attention on the monitor.

"It's important, otherwise I wouldn't bother you."

Hamson drew in a deep breath, pushed herself back from the desk and raised her eyes to Gray. "Well?"

"Not here, please."

"Ma'am and please. It must be critical."

Gray ignored the mockery. "Yes."

"Okay then." Hamson stood. "As long as it's brief."

Gray led Hamson out of the office. He entered the Major Incident Room which was currently not in use, holding the door for Hamson before closing it behind her.

"Go on." Hamson folded her arms across her chest.

"I'd appreciate your help."

Hamson laughed. Gray didn't join in. Hamson said, "You're serious? That's your opening line? No apology first?"

"I've been advised to take a friend in whenever I meet the IPCC."

"And I'm it? I'm your friend? My God, you must be desperate."

"Kind of."

"Well there's some honesty at last."

"I'm not after your job, Yvonne."

"It's ma'am, Sergeant Gray."

Gray sighed. "Okay."

"What about Mike? You guys are best buddies these days it seems."

"He can't be impartial."

"And I can?"

"More than Mike. You weren't involved."

"Is that all you two have been talking about?"

"What else would there be? Ma'am, you might be pissed off at me right now, but I believe you'd have my back."

"Like you tried to stab me in mine, you mean?"

"That's not what happened!"

"Feeling hemmed in, Sergeant? Afraid of past misdemeanours catching you out finally?"

"No, but I need someone I can trust."

"Thanks for the vote of confidence, it makes a nice change, but the answer is no. Is that everything?"

"I'd like to take a couple of days off."

"Again?"

"Carslake suggested it."

Hamson snorted. "I don't know why you bothered asking me then."

"Chain of command."

"Whatever you want, just do it," said Hamson and left the room.

Gray didn't move, considering his options. It didn't take long because there were none meaningful left. Gray had suspected Hamson would turn him down, so her doing so wasn't entirely a surprise. However, he had been hoping she'd be sufficiently neutral to put their problems aside for the moment. There was nothing else he could do, Gray had to face Smits alone. Before heading upstairs Gray collected a notebook from his desk. His coffee was at a good temperature, he drank it.

The "office" had been, as far as Gray could remember, a store room. The door was open, revealing Smits and a woman who must be Wyatt. She was younger than Smits. Her skin was very pale in contrast to her long, dark hair.

"Come in, Sergeant Gray," said Wyatt. She stood up, came around the table and offered her hand. On her wrist was a hair band. Wyatt closed the door. Smits didn't bother rising.

The interior decor was as simple as it got. A table and four chairs. Two notebooks and two pens for the investigators. An electronic tablet sat in front of Smits. Gray had expected boxes of records for the investigators to be sifting through and referring to. There weren't any. Maybe they just hadn't arrived yet. Or they had electronic copies, which Smits could access on the tablet. Smits looked like the type who'd prefer the physical form, though. To feel the old paper between his fingers and read the actual words the officers had written.

"Sit, please," said Smits. Gray did, placing his notebook down. "Do you have a representative joining you?"

"No."

"Well, it's not the end of the world, this is just a preliminary," said Wyatt with a disarming smile, warmer than Smits' earlier attempt. Gray wondered where Fowler's description of Wyatt being a cold fish had come from. She seemed amiable so far.

"May I call you Solomon?" asked Smits.

"If you want to."

"Thank you. I'm Eric, this is Emily. As I mentioned before, at this stage we're simply establishing the basic facts of the case. Hopefully this will all be over quickly, then Emily and I can go home and everything will return to normal."

"Fine." Gray took a pen out from his jacket pocket and opened up the book.

"I'm glad to hear so. Our objective is to evaluate the original decision-making process. Emily and I are one of several teams. Speaking of which, I assume you're aware of the IPCC process?"

"I am."

"Then you'll know we're here to determine whether any of the original team can be considered a witness or a person of interest."

"Okay."

"Now, at the time of the Usher case you were a DC?"

"Correct." Gray made a note of the question and his answer.

"Newly moved over, I understand."

"A few months."

"What were your initial observations when you arrived at the scene?"

"My report from the time will tell you all of this."

"I know, I'm asking for your impression. Just a broad brush to start with. A report can only tell you so much."

"We're talking about fifteen years ago."

"Correct, but I know from experience the big cases never quite leave us, do they?" Smits was basically right, though Gray wasn't going to admit that to him. "And this was your first, a special one."

"Special? In what way?"

"An unsolved homicide."

"We got a conviction."

"Rescinded now, Solomon."

"Why?"

"New evidence has come to light, making the original verdict unsafe."

"Can you be specific?"

Smits sat back, twirling his pen around his thumb like a mini baton. "The conviction hinged around material discovered under the victim's fingernails. Despite there being a report on the DNA identification of that substance, we can find no evidence it was actually submitted for analysis."

"That's news to me."

Smits and Wyatt shared a glance. "You've worked for DCI Carslake for some time now."

"From the day I joined CID."

"Is he a good boss?"

"Most of the time."

"Not all?"

"Nobody's perfect."

"How did he conduct himself during the Usher case?"

"As he always does; methodically and by the rules."

"Nothing he did gave you cause for concern?"

"No."

"Were you aware of any surveillance of Duncan Usher?"

"No, that would have been outside my pay grade."

"So neither DS Carslake nor DI Copeland, as they were then, confided in you?"

"Why would they?"

"From what I've heard, you three were a close-knit group that pretty much ran the entire investigation."

"Of a fashion."

"What does that mean?"

"DI Copeland had his own approach, the rest of us were expected to follow."

"Or suffer the consequences, we've heard."

"Maybe."

"Getting Usher's conviction was a big win for you at a very early stage of your career."

"Usher was DI Copeland's collar."

"Does that bother you?"

"We were part of a team."

"I know you weren't a fan of DI Copeland's methods."

"They got results."

"That's one way of looking at it." Smits paused for a moment or two before he said, "Do you know that there have been several investigations into DI Copeland?"

"I'd no idea. Why would I?"

"You two didn't stay in touch?"

"I haven't paid any attention to him since he moved on and vice versa."

"Glad to see the back of him?"

"Partially."

"DI Copeland maintained a network of friends and confidantes across the country – men who'd worked for him. Those whose careers he'd helped and, effectively, owed him."

"Like me you mean?"

"He gave you your shot at CID."

"I'd have got it one day anyway, I didn't feel I owed DI Copeland."

"Did he ever offer you more?"

"Promotion. And I turned him down before you ask."

"Why?"

"It would have meant uprooting my family. If that was going to happen, I'd have done so for a meaningful posting. And, as you mentioned, his methods and mine weren't compatible."

"I see from your records that your conduct is hardly unblemished."

"Is that relevant, Mr Smits?"

Smits didn't respond, instead he stared at Wyatt, seemingly trying to force a smile. The silence stretched, Gray worked hard not to fall into the trap of filling in the gap. Half a minute ticked by. Gray knew he was going to beat Smits. So did Smits.

The smile on Smits's face broadened. He turned back to Gray and said, "I think we're done for now, Sergeant. Thanks very much for your time." He stood and opened the door.

Gray headed downstairs slowly, allowing his heart rate to ease. The Detectives' Office was quiet when he entered, the atmosphere obviously tight. Hamson ignored Gray, sharply tapping on her keyboard.

Fowler sidled over to Gray's desk. He squatted down and quietly asked, "How did it go?"

"No problem, surprisingly."

"Did you expect it to be difficult?"

"I wasn't sure either way, to be honest."

"What did they ask you?"

"DS Fowler." It was Smits in the doorway to the office. He crooked his finger.

"The master calls," said Fowler.

"Good luck," Gray told him.

His phone bleeped. The text was identical to yesterday, the number blocked. It said, "You've got mail." Gray expected it would be the Usher case notes. He was keen to take a peek, but they would have to wait for tonight, when Gray's shift was over so there wasn't a trace on his work computer of data he shouldn't have.

Fifteen

Then Copeland raised his warrant card and introduced himself to the woman who answered the door. She wiped her hands on her chequered apron. She had short curly hair and a mark in the centre of her forehead. Gray wasn't sure if it was a bruise or a birth mark.

"Eva's in the living room. I'm her neighbour."

Eva Franklin slumped in a chair, legs crossed at the ankles and hands in her lap. Valerie's mother was slight and delicate looking. Eva stood when they entered, wiping the tears from her face with the back of her hands. Gray recognised her immediately from the photos in Valerie's house, though her face had sunk in on itself with grief, and her eyes were bloodshot.

Copeland introduced himself all over again, telling Eva who Gray and Carslake were too.

"I'll make you a cup of tea," said the neighbour and retreated.

"Thank you for your time, Mrs Franklin," said Copeland.

"It's Miss. I'm divorced. And it's Eva."

Pointing to a chair, Copeland said, "May we?" Eva nodded. Copeland sat on the sofa, Carslake beside him. Gray took one of the dining table chairs further back in the room so Eva didn't feel hemmed in. "I'm very sorry for your loss."

Eva's hand went to a cross hanging from a chain about her neck. "I can't believe it. I was with her a few hours ago and now she's..." Eva's voice trailed off. "How do I tell the girls? They'll be devastated."

"Where are they?"

"With Therese, Valerie's sister, a couple of doors away. They're safe."

"That's good to hear," said Carslake. "We can offer social support if that helps."

"Does anything help in times like these?"

Carslake didn't answer.

"When was the last time you saw your daughter, Mrs Franklin?" asked Copeland.

"Earlier this afternoon, when she brought the girls round."

"Was that normal? Would she often drop them off?"

"I have a very good relationship with my family, Inspector. I see the girls whenever I can, though usually with a little more notice."

"You weren't expecting them then?"

"No, but I didn't mind. They're my grandchildren, I never complain at the chance to spend time in their company. Delightful little girls."

"When was Valerie supposed to pick them up again?"

"She didn't really say."

The neighbour entered and placed a tray, laden with cups, a teapot, a plate of biscuits and a milk jug, beside Gray. "Can I leave you to play mother?" she asked Gray.

"Of course," he said. The neighbour left again. "Tea, anyone?"

Copeland and Carslake shook their heads. Gray poured himself a cup. No point letting it go to waste.

"I haven't been able to keep anything down," said Eva. "Who do you think will get custody of the children?"

"That's not really my area of expertise, Eva," said Copeland.

"He can't get them. It would be wrong."

"Mr Usher? What do you think of him?"

The irritation was clear on Eva's face the moment Copeland mentioned her son-in-law's name.

"He's poison. At first he was charming, couldn't do enough for us all. But once they were married and Val was pregnant, his true colours came out. The man was a control freak. Wanting to know where she was all the time, who she spent her time with, et cetera. It was awful. He made it hard even for me and Therese to see Val."

"What about his daughters?"

"To be fair I can't fault him there. He dotes on them. But this last year, they just became an excuse for Duncan to be round her house all the time. He wouldn't leave her alone. He was like a bee around honey. She was sick of it."

"Mr Usher told us earlier he and your daughter were moving back in together."

Eva frowned. "That makes no sense." She shook her head. "Val was seeing someone else."

"Who?"

"She wouldn't say. She did tell me he'd be moving in with her. Once he'd got divorced."

"Her new partner was married?"

"That's how I understood it."

"What was Mr Usher's reaction when he found out his wife was in another relationship?"

"He was incandescent, Inspector." Eva grinned briefly at the memory, but there was no humour within. "Ultimately that's why Duncan wouldn't leave her alone. He couldn't stand it. He lost his temper several times, right in front of me. One moment he was calm, the next he exploded into anger. It was frightening. And now my daughter is dead." Eva leaned over. "It's all his fault. He killed her!"

Eva slumped back, her anger spent.

"I've a request to make of you, Eva. I'm sorry to do this, but Valerie's body needs identifying. Either by you or your daughter, we don't mind."

Eva closed her eyes, slumped back in her chair. "I'll do it," she whispered. "She's my child."

"I TOLD YOU THIS INVOLVED Usher somehow," said Copeland when they were standing on the pavement outside Eva's house.

"Certainly seems that way, sir," said Carslake.

Gray was taken aback. "The evidence is circumstantial surely, sir."

"We have a motive now, constable. Usher's wife was screwing another man. 'Incandescent,' Eva said. Prone to losing his temper. Remember how Valerie died? Strangled in the heat of the moment. That's his rage and anger coming out, son." Copeland looked over the Carslake. "Jeff, lean on the lab for those results. Don't forget to say I want them; a bit of seniority always helps. And have a word with Jenkinson. See when the PM is. I want you both there for the results, okay?"

Sixteen

Now When Gray was inside his flat, he pulled out his laptop fired it up, and opened up his personal email account. The note from Pennance was awaiting him. Gray clicked on it.

Within the body was a single embedded link. Another click opened a page with a series of directories. Gray randomly picked one, producing a list of files.

Gray hovered the mouse arrow over a filename. It struck Gray that he was about to break the rules again, like when he'd amassed every document he could on Tom's disappearance, whether he was allowed to have them or not.

He clicked anyway and was looking at a scanned copy of a post mortem report written by the pathologist Amos Jenkinson.

At this rate it would take days to go over everything. The volume of data was massive. It had been a significant case, with a large team, all contributing information. Focus. He needed to focus. The trouble was, he wasn't sure what on. The only clue he had was from Smits – the finger pointed at the DNA evidence. Gray made a pot of coffee. He was going to be in for a long night.

He started at the beginning, with his own account from the evening as first responder. It was strange, going over the document. It was familiar, yet it felt like someone else's words.

There was a naïve honesty about them. Then he shifted to Jenkinson's reports. They appeared perfectly reasonable to Gray, nothing within made him doubt the pathologist's statements.

After over an hour staring at the laptop, Gray sat back and rubbed his eyes. He headed out onto the balcony and stared out over the black sea. It was a clear night. He could see the winking red and white lights on the horizon, marking the European coast. Not so far away. *Where Tom possibly was*. Gray thought about Carslake's suggestion that the trail had reached Amsterdam. He wasn't entirely sure Carslake was telling the truth. Intentional or not, Carslake had ushered Gray down a cold trail before.

At least one of Carslake's tips had led Gray to Inspector Jacques Morel in Calais, who had processed a report of someone with Tom's description. Gray had stayed in touch with his French counterpart, who had recently been promoted to Chief Inspector and relocated to Lyon. Gray had come to like the gruff Frenchman, and Morel had carried on hunting for Tom. However, the move upwards meant Morel had even less time to help. All he'd uncovered so far was a blank. Gray had fed Carslake's assertion about the possible sighting in Holland to Morel, though he hadn't got a response yet. But Gray remained hopeful. He had to. He'd been searching for his missing years. He couldn't give up now.

With a deep inhale of salty sea air, he went back inside and woke up the laptop. There was one unresolved strand of the case that still bothered him today. The identity of Valerie's lover. Copeland had considered the information peripheral and Carslake had agreed. Back then, as just a DC, he hadn't been able to sway either of his superior officers otherwise. The

Crown Prosecution Service was happy with the case as present-
ed to them. And Usher had been found unanimously guilty;
Copeland's approach and belief vindicated.

But not anymore.

The obvious next step was to speak with the now-retired
Jenkinson. The pair had stayed in touch infrequently. Gray
looked at his watch. It was late, but he still had work to do. He
clicked on a folder and found Carslake's notes. Several pages
in he felt himself beginning to nod. His eyelids were drooping,
and his head felt too heavy for his neck. He reluctantly decided
to finish the report he was on, then call it a night.

Another couple of paragraphs on, something caught Gray's
attention. Gray sat up and shifted his eyes back to the top of the
page. *This must be some sort of mistake.* He scanned the section
again. When his consciousness finally caught up, he jolted fully awake. He re-read Carslake's words over and over. No matter
how many times he did, the outcome was the same. *They were
a lie.* The alterations were subtle and would only be spotted by
someone with first-hand experience of the case. Of which there
were only a handful of people.

Gray picked up his mobile and dialled Pennance. He answered within a few rings, sounding groggy. "It's late, Sol. What
this time?"

Gray didn't care he'd woken Pennance. "The Usher case
notes. Where did you get them?"

"This was supposed to be a no-questions-asked kind of
deal, remember?"

"Where?" urged Gray.

"From HOLMES, of course." An acronym for the second
iteration of the "Home Office Large Major Enquiry System".

"Sol, what's up?"

"I don't know yet," lied Gray. He was in trouble, big trouble, if the IPCC had tripped over the same inconsistencies. There was a chance they hadn't, but Gray needed to assume the worst case. "I need a couple of contact details."

"And you can't get them yourself, because?"

"No records." Gray could easily search for the information, though by doing so he'd leave an electronic trail. "I want to reach my old boss. He was the SIO on the case."

"Copeland."

"Right. And Craig Mundby, who was a victim. Last I knew he lived with James and Molly Mundby."

"I already have Copeland's details. I thought you'd ask me at some point. Ever been to Carlisle?"

"Never had the need to."

"It's the capital of Cumbria."

"I know that much."

"It's where Copeland's living now. Actually in a village five miles outside Carlisle called Wetheral. Rather exclusive, I understand. He reached the rank of DCI before retiring last year."

"Copeland always knew he'd go far."

"Well he did. A couple of pointers that might be useful to you. Your friend hasn't been so successful in his personal life as at work. He's on his third marriage, she's called Sarah. A couple of business ventures he was involved in went south too."

"Good to know, thanks."

"No problem. Enjoy your trip down memory lane."

Pennance rang off. Gray headed out onto the balcony and listened to the waves while he thought about what he'd read. If the IPCC had picked up on the same subtleties they'd have him in their sights. And there were only two people who could have set him up.

Carslake or Copeland.

Gray decided he'd go see Jenkinson first, then pay his old boss a visit.

Seventeen

Then

The length of Jenkinson's working day since Valerie's body had been discovered was etched onto his face. Black shadows under his eyes, ruffled hair, wrinkled clothes. And a deep yawn. Carslake, sitting next to Gray, had a similar appearance. Gray didn't feel much better; he'd only grabbed a snatched nap and a change of clothes himself. He hadn't seen Kate or the kids, arriving home after they were in bed and rising again before they did.

After a few hours' sleep Jenkinson had proceeded with the post mortem. Copeland was keen to get some answers, and he would work everyone as hard as possible, himself included, to ensure he got them.

The pathologist sagged into the chair in his small office and rubbed the bridge of his nose. There was barely enough room for the two visitors' seats which Gray and Carslake occupied. A soft light was finding its way through the windows set high in the wall. A lamp on Jenkinson's desk was on, though it still felt gloomy. Several coffee cups littered the surface of the desk.

"It's all in there," said Jenkinson, holding out a folder.

"Thanks, Amos." Carslake took the document. He began to flip through the contents. "Copeland won't wait to read it, and I won't have the time to before he'll be on at me. What are the key points?"

"I'm dead on my feet here. The man's a slave driver, you know that?"

"All too well. The sooner you tell us, the sooner we're gone."

"Bluntly, Mrs Usher quite unusually died from a cardiac inhibition as a result of manual strangulation. I've included a number of photographs to support my hypothesis. In terms of procedure I focused on the neck area, of course, removing the larynx and hyoid bone, keeping the tongue attached."

"Must you?" interrupted Carslake.

"Yes. Feel free to look at the photos if you like, they're quite instructive."

Gray took the report from Carslake's fingers. He barely noticed. First was a full length shot of the body, the second a close up of the throat, pre-incision. From there the content became more graphic. Gray stared at the images, one after the other.

When Carslake didn't answer, Jenkinson carried on. "I examined the superficial and deep musculature of the neck for contusion haemorrhage, then moved onto the laryngeal skeleton before exposing the laryngeal skeleton for fractures. I'd say first the killer applied sufficient pressure on the victim's neck to obstruct the carotid arteries, preventing blood flow from the brain. There were bruises evident on the skin and in the internal neck tissues and bleeding of the larynx to indicate this. When I examined Mrs Usher's brain, I discovered signs of anoxic encephalopathy – dead cells basically, resulting from oxygen starvation."

"Brain damage?" asked Gray. Carslake had retreated into himself.

"Eloquently put, Sol, yes. At this point, even if she'd survived, her faculties would have been severely compromised.

However, her attacker probably shifted his grip onto the carotid artery nerve ganglion which would have resulted in the cardiac arrest."

"You said that's uncommon?"

"Oh yes."

"Why?"

"The force must be applied to a very specific and rather small area of the throat."

"Do you think it was deliberate?"

Jenkinson shrugged. "You'll have to ask the killer. It could have happened by pure chance." Jenkinson picked up one of the coffee mugs and took a pull. He grimaced. "Her death would not have been quick. I'd have expected her to have fought back, although I also found a mark on her cheek which could indicate she was hit first which may have stunned her. I've scraped under her fingernails. If we're lucky there'll be some organic material we can identify."

"That's great news," said Carslake.

"It's not the only information I gleaned. There were clear signs that Mrs Usher had sex shortly before her death. No semen though so either he didn't finish or he used a condom. DNA can only be found in sperm cells, not the fluid itself. So no ejaculation, no DNA."

"Did you check for pubic hairs?" asked Gray.

"Of course, and no, I didn't find any."

"Unusual."

"Yes. It's as if someone removed all traces of themselves."

"Thorough, as always, Amos," said Carslake.

"It's what I'm here for."

"We'll get out of your way."

"I'll be getting some well-earned rest. Close the door on your way out, would you?" Jenkinson settled further into his chair, put his feet up on his desk and closed his eyes. Gray did as Jenkinson asked.

Before Gray could ask his boss why he hadn't tabled more questions, Carslake's mobile rang. Carslake listened briefly.

"Are you all right?" asked Gray.

"Craig Mundby's awake."

Eighteen

Now Amos Jenkinson had retired to a red-brick barn conversion nestled in the village of Fordwich just off the Canterbury road. A couple of thousand years ago Fordwich was a major port, but the gradual silting up of the River Stour meant it was now landlocked. Jenkinson's home was on the edge of the village, at the end of a cul-de-sac with fields to the rear. Gray parked on the drive. He could still hear the traffic making its way in and out of the city.

Gray rang the bell. A short woman of about Gray's age answered the door. Her hair was long and grey, tumbling past her shoulders. Large, elaborate earrings dangled from her lobes, almost long enough to touch her shoulder. "Can I help you?"

"Is Amos in?"

"My father's resting right now. Who are you?"

"Sorry, I'm Solomon Gray, an ex-colleague of his."

"Sol!" A voice bellowed from inside the home. Jenkinson was standing in the hallway behind his daughter. He looked frail and bent; he was using a metal framed walker to keep himself upright. He still wore the over-sized, pork-chop sideburns.

"Dad, you're supposed to be in bed!"

"I'll be dead soon, why would I waste time lying down?"

"You'll tire yourself out."

"I'm fine, Fiona. Don't fuss." Jenkinson switched his attention to Gray. "Come in, Sol. Fiona shouldn't have left you standing on the step. Fancy a drink?"

Jenkinson turned slowly around before Gray could answer, shuffling along the hall, pushing the walker out in front of him an arm's length then sliding his feet forward. It was a slow process. Jenkinson led Gray and his daughter into a conservatory which opened out onto a garden of long grass and mature trees. A pair of French windows stood open, letting the cool air in. Several pieces of wicker furniture, bedecked with floral cushions, faced outwards. Jenkinson paused by a table on which stood multiple bottles and glasses.

"What's your poison, Sol?" he asked.

"Dad!"

"I don't want another cup of tea, Fiona. I'm drowning in the bloody stuff. Sol is an old friend, so I'll be having some of the hard stuff. You can leave us to it." Fiona turned around and walked out. Jenkinson waited until she was out of earshot before he said, "She fusses so much."

"Probably because she cares."

Jenkinson shrugged. "Whisky or brandy?"

"I'm driving Amos, and I'm on duty."

"Balls, man! The years have made you soft. Have a bloody drink with me!" Jenkinson sloshed some whisky into a glass, added a dribble of water and pressed it into Gray's hand. "Sit down."

Gray did so and shortly Jenkinson joined him. He eased himself down, pushed the walker away and took a swallow from a considerably larger measure.

"How are you then, Sol? It's been a long time."

"Okay. How about you?"

Jenkinson swirled the booze in the glass, staring into it. "I've got early onset Alzheimer's. And arthritis to add insult to injury. But that won't matter because once my brain goes, the body forgets how to live."

"I'm sorry, Amos."

"There's nothing can be done. So to warn you, I have a tendency to forget recent events. I have good days and bad."

"I'm here about the past."

"I rather thought you might be. Duncan Usher by any chance?"

"There's an internal investigation underway."

"Of course there is. This bloody desire to wring our hands then hold them out to be slapped by the public – it's irritating and it's wrong."

"No argument from me, Amos."

"There's been a letter already. From somebody called Smits."

"I met him yesterday."

"And?"

"It's why I'm here. There seems to be some doubt about the DNA analysis on the material you found under Valerie's nails."

"Hmm, that's what they're focusing on, is it?"

"To be honest I don't know the breadth of their assessment."

"Well they're going to have a bloody job proving anything, and soon I won't remember at all." Jenkinson threw the rest of the alcohol down his throat. "The data went missing, destroyed after the case was closed."

Gray was puzzled, critical information was supposed to be retained following the conclusion of a case, regardless of outcome. "What about the sample itself? The analysis could be re-run, surely?"

"Yes, if it existed. A freezer broke down. Nobody noticed until it was too late. Valerie's material was just one of many that were lost."

"That's unfortunate."

"It's more than unfortunate, Sol. What's the chances of both the data and the sample being unavailable for further examination?"

"Slim."

"At best."

"Somebody didn't want the work being carried out."

"Who?"

"Copeland. And I can prove it. Give me a hand, would you?" Jenkinson held out his arms to be pulled up.

Gray put his untouched drink down on the floor and obliged Jenkinson.

"I get sick of that damned walker. If you don't mind, I'll lean on you instead."

"No problem. Where are we going?"

"My study, it's just back down the hall. Second door along." They exited the conservatory and returned the way they'd come.

Fiona appeared in the corridor. "Is everything all right?"

"Fine, fine." Jenkinson waved her away.

Gray pushed the door open, revealing a well organised space, a desk in the central area before the window, shelves and filing cabinets either side. There were medical certificates on the wall and, for some reason, what appeared to be an African tribal shield crossed with two spears.

"You go in, I'll stay here," said Jenkinson, propping himself up against the jamb.

"What am I looking for?"

"Filing cabinet, bottom drawer over there."

Gray followed Jenkinson's bony finger, which pointed in the general direction. Within the cabinet were alphabetised sections from U to Z. U was the thickest.

"Look for Usher," said Jenkinson.

Gray pulled out the sheaf and closed the drawer. It was a requisition for Jenkinson's post mortem, bloods, and any other documentation Jenkinson had produced in the process of assessing the murder of Valerie Usher and dated a year after Usher's successful conviction.

"Did you comply?" asked Gray.

"Of course!" Gray was wasn't surprised. "Will you be talking to Copeland?"

"Yes, don't you worry, Amos."

Jenkinson grinned, looking more like his old self. "Good. One thing I remember with clarity is that I never liked that bastard."

GRAY LEFT JENKINSON in the conservatory, the bottle of whisky beside him and one of his business cards, should Jenkinson recall anything else of value. They'd spent a good half an hour going over old times. Clearly the pathologist missed his old life. Stuck, as Jenkinson had put it, in a ramshackle house staring out at the world as it passed him by.

At the front door Fiona stepped into the hall.

"He's resting," said Gray.

"The silly old sod will have worn himself out," she said. "He's not had this much adventure in ages."

"He said he has Alzheimer's."

"Yes, some rare form. So far it's not so bad but the experts say it's a steep downhill slope."

"How long?"

Fiona's mouth turned down. "Months."

There was nothing Gray could say other than goodbye.

Nineteen

T**hen**
It was obvious which hospital room along the corridor was Craig Mundby's. Two uniformed cops flanked either side of the door. Both had been immediate colleagues of Gray's until his move to CID.

"Take a break," Carslake told them.

"Thanks, sir."

"Bring us all a tea back, would you?"

"It's crap, sir."

"Like the wife, as long as it's hot and wet it'll be fine."

The PCs grinned while Carslake, damn him, chuckled. Gray kept his face straight. The joke wasn't amusing in the slightest.

Gray followed Carslake into the private room. He closed the door behind them. Craig Mundby lay propped up in bed. His round face was as pale as the sheets his bandaged wrists lay on.

Craig wasn't alone. A man and a woman sat in chairs either side of the bed. She looked like she hadn't slept all night, greying hair pulled up into a messy bun, her face etched with worried lines. She cradled Craig's hand within her own. The man was at least a decade younger. He looked like a surfer; sandy unkempt hair, tanned skin. A necklace of beads hung around his neck; a similar arrangement on his wrist.

126

"Don't get up," said Carslake when the man made to stand. "DS Carslake and DC Gray."

"I'm Molly Mundby, and this is my husband, James."

"We're investigating the murder of Valerie Usher, and we need to understand the part Craig played in all of this."

"Craig can't have killed her." Molly shook her head emphatically. "He can't even have been involved, officer."

"Ms Mundby," Carslake ventured slowly. "Your son was found on the floor next to Mrs Usher's corpse."

"He wouldn't hurt anybody, just the opposite. He's the protective sort."

"He just likes to be friends," said James.

There was a knock at the door. One of the uniforms entered with a tray of tea in paper cups. Carslake took the drinks, and the uniform left. Gray declined the offer, as did Molly. James accepted and sat holding the cup in both hands, staring into its depths.

"Craig works for James," said Molly. "Nobody else would employ him."

"Why would that be?"

"Craig's a tactile lad," said James, "though not everybody appreciates it."

"We've always done the gardens at the house," said Molly. "We're friends with the owners, and we live close by, on Bishop Avenue, so it's easy to pop over regularly and keep on top of the greenery."

Gray knew Bishop Avenue. It adjoined Castle Avenue, the street on which Valerie's house stood. It was just a few minutes' walk away.

"The house doesn't belong to Mrs Usher?" asked Gray.

"No, she leases it. Moved in a few months ago. Basically James and Craig come with the place. They were there yesterday, weren't you love? Sorting out the borders."

James nodded. "Some shrubs needed cutting back, and the lawn was due for a final mow. Still lots of growth, even at this time of year."

"Did you see Mrs Usher?"

"Yes, she always comes out to say hello to both of us."

"What about the girls?"

"They were running around the back garden while we worked. Val shouted at them to come inside."

"Val? Were you two friends?"

Molly, frowning, said, "James just cuts the grass."

"Mr Mundby?" asked Carslake.

"We weren't familiar, no."

"Was there any interaction between Mrs Usher and Craig?"

"She just said hello."

"How did she seem to you?"

"All she said was hello, Sergeant!" said Molly.

"Normal," said James, pursing his lips.

"And Duncan Usher, did you see him?"

"He came out into the garden with the girls. The four of them played catch while I pruned."

"Craig and Duncan got on well?" asked Gray.

"Craig gets on with everyone, Sergeant," said Molly.

"Earlier your husband said not everybody appreciates Craig's tactile nature."

"But they like him."

"Have you got a key to the property, Mr Mundby?"

"No, he doesn't."

"Constable Gray asked your husband the question, Mrs Mundby," said Carslake. Molly folded her arms.

"I don't have any keys to anywhere. Val – Mrs Usher – sorry, makes sure everything is unlocked for us when we arrive. I access the back garden through the side gate."

"What about the house?" asked Gray.

"No, why would I? We keep all our tools in the garden shed."

"Did Mrs Usher keep the front gate open while you were there?"

"It's always closed."

"Always?"

"Yes."

"When did you finish?" asked Carslake.

"Mid-afternoon, about 3 p.m. I'd guess. It was a beautiful day, and Mr Usher let us knock off early. I took Craig for a pint."

"Where?"

"The Albion, on the sea front."

"It's not the nearest pub."

"I know, but you can't beat the view."

Gray made a note to get confirmation of the Mundbys' presence. It was a busy hotel with a popular bar, even more so on a sunny day.

"Then what?" asked Carslake.

"We went home, had dinner."

"And Craig came home with you?"

"That's right."

"When did you realise Craig was missing?" asked Carslake.

"Not until just before your colleague rang," said Molly. Craig went to his room to play on his game console after we'd eaten. I went to check on him, but he wasn't there. He'd climbed out the window."

"Had he done that before?"

"I don't think so."

"Do you always check on your son at night?"

"More often than not."

"Why?"

"Because he's my son."

"Why would Craig be at Mrs Usher's?"

"Has something happened to Valerie?" asked Craig, now awake, cutting off Molly before she could answer. He blinked repeatedly as if the light was too bright for him. Molly stood and closed the curtains. He looked around the room before lifting a bandaged wrist up and staring at it. "What happened?"

"Valerie's dead, Craig," said Molly gently. "The police are here to find out what happened to her."

"Dead? How?"

"What do you remember about last night?" asked Carslake. Craig had been staring at his mother, but his attention shifted to Carslake, who Craig seemed to see for the first time. His eyes widened.

"Now's not the time, Sergeant," said Molly.

"Mrs Mundby, we're investigating a murder." Carslake switched his attention to Craig again.

Craig stared at her until Molly reluctantly nodded. "Go on, Craig."

He thought hard, the concentration clear on his face. "Playing Sonic The Hedgehog."

"What time did you go to bed?"

"I don't know." Craig turned away.

"Craig," pushed Molly.

"Late."

"You were found in Mrs Usher's house this morning," said Carslake. "How did you get there?"

"I just ... I don't know." Craig appeared confused, his eyelids blinking rapidly again, breathing shallow.

"It's all right, Craig," said Molly, gripping his hand and stroking his head.

"Mum?"

"You were found beside Mrs Usher's bed," said Carslake, "Your wrists slashed."

"No." Craig lifted his arm once more, staring down at the bandages, the same expression of puzzlement and confusion on his face.

"How did you get there, Craig?"

"I don't understand. I don't know. She can't be dead. She's my friend!"

"Stop this, Sergeant Carslake! You're upsetting my son."

"We're investigating a murder, Mrs Mundby."

"I just do the gardens with James. I don't remember anything. One minute I was playing games in my room, the next I woke up in here. I don't know what you're talking about!"

"He's already said he didn't do it, Sergeant," said Molly.

"Mrs Mundby, please. Have you anything else to say Craig?"

"I don't remember what happened. I promise!"

"Okay, Craig," said Gray. "If you remember anything ask one of the officers outside to give me or Sergeant Carslake a

call. And we'll have to talk again when you're feeling up to it."
Craig nodded, lay back and closed his eyes.

"Can we have a word outside, Mrs Mundby?" Molly followed Carslake and Gray into the corridor. Once Gray had
closed the door Carslake said, "I'd like to take a DNA sample
from Craig."

"Why?"

"For elimination purposes. It's voluntary, of course."

"We've nothing to hide, feel free."

"Thank you. Constable Gray will be back shortly."

Molly went back inside.

"What do you think to all of that?" asked Gray.

"Hard to be sure," said Carslake. "At best Craig is an unreli-
able witness. Bit of tension between man and wife as well. Why
doesn't Craig remember what happened?"

"Trauma?"

"There's a lot Mrs Mundby isn't telling us. Did you see
how keen she was to step in whenever her husband opened his
mouth to speak?"

"It was hard to miss."

"Anyway, I'd better call Copeland and give him an update.
Take a DNA swab from Craig while I do that, would you, Sol?"

Before Gray could answer Carslake was walking away and
tugging the phone from his pocket.

Twenty

N^{ow} Gray took the first available train to Wetheral, changing in London before heading for the north west. Not as great a distance as to Edinburgh, but it took longer because the train was slower and stopped at more stations.

It was late afternoon by the time Gray arrived, carrying the same bag he'd lugged to Edinburgh. He had a couple of days' holiday, so that's what he was doing. If he happened to spend it with their old boss, where was the harm in that? Copeland was the fulcrum around which the Usher case revolved – he had been fifteen years ago and he would be now. Copeland was that kind of man.

Gray stepped onto the platform at Wetheral. According to the village website, the settlement on the River Eden was "picturesque". Gray wasn't here for the view, but as he exited the station, he could see why Copeland had selected it. Plenty of green, rolling hills in the distance, and it was peaceful. He'd booked a room just yards away station, in a pub called The Crown, rambling and whitewashed, standing on a narrow road. Gray walked over and checked in.

Upstairs in his room, he sat on the bed. A few days ago he was in Scotland, today he was only ten miles from the border, but on the Western side of the country. The constant bustle was wearing him thin. He felt like lying down and getting a few hours' rest. But his objective was Copeland, and that couldn't wait. Gray was going to catch his old boss unawares.

According to the map on Gray's phone, Copeland's address was just around the corner. Gray followed the route until he reached his destination, a house almost as large as the pub and facing an extensive village green. He stood on the pavement and looked it over. Copeland had done well for himself. The detached, solidly built house stood in an expanse of well-tended land with mature trees and borders. Two cars were on the drive, both Mercedes, relatively new and highly specified. A large 4x4 and a smaller soft-top two-seater.

Retirement for Copeland brought a generous lump sum and an annual pension. Way more than Gray would achieve if he stuck at sergeant. He thought again about what Carslake had said about an inspector's position and the benefits it would bring. Gray wasn't sure whether he wanted to pay the price to get it, though.

He walked up the drive, feet scrunching in pebbles. The front door was painted a glossy black, inset with frosted panes of glass, etched with fleur de lys. Large bay windows pressed out either side. A long brass handle hung down beside the door. Gray tugged on it, and a bell rang somewhere deep within.

After a few moments a shadow fell across the glass, and door opened. This must be Copeland's wife, Sarah. She smiled, trusting and friendly. Gray reckoned she was early fifties, younger than Copeland; curly ginger hair fell to her shoulders, green eyes.

"Hello," said Gray. "Solomon Gray. Terry and I used to work together. Is he available?"

"He's in his study. Come in." She opened the door wider and Gray stepped into a brightly lit hallway. "Can I take your coat?"

Gray shrugged his jacket off, and Sarah hung it up on a stand which appeared to be antique. Several walking sticks stood against it. A couple of Barbour jackets and a flat cap hung from hooks.

"Where were you and Terry based?" asked Sarah. "I don't think we've met before."

"Kent."

Sarah frowned, thinking. "That would have been a while ago then. Before me."

"About fifteen years."

"What brings you here after all that time?"

"I'm on holiday in the area. A mutual friend said this was where Terry lived now. Jeff Carslake."

She nodded, no apparent recognition of Carslake's name. "The study is just down here." Sarah led him along a corridor. The decor was stripped and varnished wood, white-painted walls; very traditional. Sarah paused before a door, knocked then entered. Gray followed.

Copeland sat at a roll-top desk facing an expansive window which looked out onto the garden. He half turned in his seat. An imminent expression of irritation, his mouth opening to voice a complaint, turned to one of surprise with perhaps a touch of fear as Sarah said, "An old friend to see you."

Copeland stood, his lips twisting into a smile devoid of pleasure. "Solomon Gray, as I live and breathe." He took Gray's hand and pumped it furiously. "Sol and I used to be colleagues."

"I know," said Sarah, "he told me. I'll bring you two a drink."

"Great, thanks," said Gray.

Sarah left, closing the door behind her.

"What the hell are you doing here?" Copeland demanded.

"Nice to see you too, Terry." Gray glanced around the room. Two walls were full of books, floor to ceiling. The remaining walls were replete with paintings of hunting and shooting. A fireplace with tiled surround was the main feature. Very much the country look. Copeland himself was dressed in suitable attire for the outdoor life in tweed plus fours, knee-length thick socks and a white shirt. Copeland's wavy hair remained suspiciously dark, so he probably dyed it periodically. His face, however, displayed Copeland's age – saggy jowls and a deeply lined forehead.

"As I told your wife," Gray said. "I'm on holiday in the area and thought I'd look up an old friend."

Copeland eyed Gray. "Any pretence at friendship ended when you walked out on me."

"And I've never regretted that. It's about Usher."

"Not here." Copeland left the study, clearly expecting Gray to follow. He turned towards the rear of the house. At the end of the corridor was a large kitchen, also traditional. An Aga cooker inset into an old fireplace; beams and cupboard painted French grey. Sarah was working a coffee machine which was erupting steam into the room.

"We're going outside," said Copeland.

Two dogs, pointers Gray thought, were asleep in baskets by the back door. At his voice the dogs leapt up, heads raised to their master, waiting to see what he wanted them to do. Gray couldn't shake how much their pose reflected that of the men Copeland had commanded when he was still in the police.

"You might as well take this with you," said Sarah, holding a tray with two small cups and saucers, a milk jug and sugar bowl on it. Gray took the tray. Copeland waited for Gray to exit, then threw the ball for the dogs who dashed off after it.

"I'll join you in a moment," said Copeland and closed the door. Gray crossed the expanse of grass to a cast-iron set of table and chairs and put the tray down. One of the dogs had retrieved the ball. Gray held out his hand and the dog released it into his palm. It was wet with saliva. Gray threw the ball. While both dogs chased after it, Gray wiped his hand on the back of his trousers.

By the time Copeland came into the garden, Gray had thrown the ball four times, drunk a cup of coffee, and the rest had gone cold.

Copeland approached the table, and stared at Gray through narrowed eyes. "How dare you come here, Sergeant," said Copeland. His soft tone clashed with the expression of rage on his face. Copeland was back to his old self.

"You're not my commanding officer anymore," said Gray. "Only one of us is still a serving officer."

"That's correct, but I'd bet a month of your wages that I have substantially more influence in the ranks than you do." The dogs competed for the ball; the winner returned and dropped it at Copeland's feet. He threw it.

"Is that a threat?"

"Take it any way you want."

"An approach like yours, Terry, only works if the person you're attempting to intimidate actually gives a shit. There was a time I'd have listened to you, but that was long ago when I was fresh and impressionable. I'm older and much more cynical these days."

Copeland glared at Gray, his jaw working. "Has Carslake sanctioned your trip?"

"Not as such, no."

"Some honesty for once. I called Jeff just now. He had no idea you were here."

"You told him?" Gray couldn't keep the concern out of his voice. He leaned forward in his chair, searching Copeland's face for more information.

Copeland smiled, and pulled out the chair to sit. "No, but your reaction explains a hell of a lot. So what do you want? Speak your piece, then fuck off."

"Usher's out."

"I'm well aware of his movements. I still have friends, you know." Gray's mobile rang in his pocket. He ignored it. They'd leave a message if it was important. "I had you pegged for a higher station than sergeant."

"Not everyone strives to reach the peak, Terry."

Copeland bristled at the continued use of his first name. "And not everyone is capable. Cream always rises."

"Sometimes it curdles."

"Oh dear, Solomon, that's a terrible analogy."

"I guess you've been expecting a visitor?"

"I thought something would occur. It was bound to the moment Usher walked free. I was SIO. I doubt there's anything I can help you with, frankly. We did everything we needed to fifteen years ago."

"So why is he free?"

Copeland shrugged. "I understand it's on the basis of a technicality."

"And a pretty big one, which seems to be down to you. Did you order evidence to be destroyed?"

"What are you talking about?" Copeland frowned.

"I saw Amos Jenkinson yesterday. He showed me an official document, signed by you, requisitioning any and all material pertaining to Valerie Usher."

"When was this?"

"Early April, around the time Usher was convicted."

"That would have been about the time I was leaving Thanet CID."

Gray stayed silent, allowed Copeland to think back. "Why would I eliminate evidence?" he asked eventually.

"Because you wanted Usher to be guilty."

"We put the right man away, Sergeant Gray. If that's being questioned now, so be it. My conscience is clear."

"I think you were so keen to get Usher, you cut corners. Isn't that right, Chief Inspector? I felt so at the time, even more so now."

"You know, Gray," Copeland leaned back and crossed his arms over his chest, "I had high hopes for you. I credited you could with the ability to be moulded into a decent copper, but you chose not to listen to my advice and go your own way. And look where that's got you."

"Unlike you."

"What do you mean?"

"A near bankrupt on his third marriage. Congratulations."

Copeland's eyes widened in surprise, but he quickly regained his composure.

"Believe it or not, Terry, I have friends too. There's an investigation into how the Usher case was handled."

"Eric Smits is running it. He's very competent."

"Does his ability bother you?"

"Not really."

But Gray thought Copeland was lying, still shaken by Gray's ambush, and his guard had dropped slightly. "Enquiries always turn up some form of dirt," said Gray. "Are you prepared for that? For your retirement to be affected?"

The kitchen door opened and Sarah shouted, "I'm going out, Terry."

Copeland waved. "Let's go back inside, it's getting cold." Gray followed Copeland.

In the kitchen the dogs settled back into their baskets and fell asleep.

"Do you want another one?" asked Copeland.

"Sure."

While Copeland busied himself with the coffee machine, Gray glanced around the room. He saw some photos on the wall. They were of two children, teenagers.

"They're Sarah's," said Copeland, "from her first marriage. He died, left Sarah his business." Copeland handed Gray a steaming cup. "Look, we got off on the wrong foot here, Sol."

"When? Today or fifteen years ago?"

"We should help each other."

"You've already told me you did nothing wrong."

"But equally you pointed out an investigation always uncovers some level of dirt. You're absolutely correct."

"Is there dirt to be found, Terry?"

"Listen, I did what I thought was right at the time. But we live in different times now, and the decisions made back then might be looked upon in a new light. And who says you're entirely clean?"

"What are you getting at?"

"Why are you here, Sol?"

"According to some people, we jailed the wrong man for Valerie Usher's murder. I'm trying to get to the bottom of what happened."

Copeland sighed. "You were right. What you said earlier. I don't have much left. A reputation, perhaps, though even that is fading. It's incredible how quickly you're forgotten once you leave. The money – Sarah's money – bought the house, the cars. She bailed me out of debt a few years ago when a business venture went south. If I blow it again, she'll leave me. And then what will I have? Not a lot."

"That's hardly my problem."

"I know. I also know you've never liked me."

"Not true. I didn't mind you at first. But as time went on, less so."

"I was good at what I did."

"I never doubted that, just your methods."

"It's why I was sent to Thanet," said Copeland. "It was either him or my job."

"So you fitted Usher up."

"No." Copeland curled his hands into fists. "I never broke the rules. I genuinely believed Usher was the culprit."

"You saw what you wanted to."

"Maybe."

"Certainly." Gray shook his head.

"I'll tell you some things, though only if you guarantee my name will be kept out of it."

"You said you know Smits. Why not tell him yourself?"

"He doesn't work that way. Our Eric is incorruptible."

Gray remembered Usher's comment from a couple of days ago. Everybody had their pressure points.

"Do you agree?"

"Tell me first, then maybe I'll agree."

Copeland clenched his jaw. Gray heard his teeth grind. "My specific task was to clean Thanet up, to take Duncan Usher down. At first I made no progress at all. I was under increasing pressure from the top to get into Usher's gang. Then we had a breakthrough. We got one, then two informants on board. People right at the heart of his activities. The intelligence was golden. I was building a cast-iron case against Usher. Then his wife got killed."

"Why not arrest him then on the basis of what you had from the surveillance?"

"It was too early in the process. He'd have been out in a few years. With a murder conviction, he'd go down for good. And it worked. Life for Usher and the gang split up. It was a hell of a coup."

"In the short term. McGavin stayed loose, and before long it was business as usual. We believe Usher carried on running the business from his cell."

"I did as much as I could."

"Who were the informants?"

"That's the problem," Copeland stared him straight in the eyes. "I don't know."

"How's that possible?"

"Their handler kept their identities to himself. He said it was safer that way. To protect them. Because otherwise Usher would find out. We had pretty good evidence Usher had various officers in his pocket. So I agreed to it. And before you ask, I was desperate."

"Who was the handler?"

"Finally Solomon, you ask the million-dollar question." Copeland clapped theatrically. "It was Jeff Carslake."

"I never knew."

"You were a DC, why should you?"

Gray swallowed half his cup of coffee while he thought through Copeland's revelation. "Could one of the informants have been Valerie?"

"I wondered the same, but only afterwards, when the case was done. It would have been a very strong motive. What's clear, Sergeant Gray, is you and I have one last case to solve together. Do so, and we save each other. Fail, and we are both in deep shit. Are you with me?"

"I don't have a lot of choice now, do I?"

"Good. I'm going to take the dogs out for a march, do you want to come along? There's plenty more to discuss."

Gray couldn't face the exertion. He was tired from the trip. "I'll pass."

"Where are you staying?"

"The Crown."

"That's where I always finish my route. How about I buy you a pint in about an hour?"

Twenty One

Then Carslake waited. As he'd arranged, Molly Mundby left her son's room, mobile in hand. It would be Copeland, asking to speak with her. One of the PCs intercepted her as she exited. She frowned, but whatever the PC said worked because she moved along the corridor to the waiting area.

Carslake caught the eye of the remaining PC and nodded. The officer entered Craig's room, came back out again moments later with James in tow, and headed in the opposite direction to Molly.

When they were gone, Carslake made his move. He wouldn't have long, a few minutes at best. Craig was still lying in bed, staring out the window. When Carslake entered, Craig looked to the door. A blank expression on his face turned to concern then panic.

"My parents aren't here," said Craig.

"That's okay," said Carslake, "it's you I want. We've got a bit of a problem, you and I, don't we?"

"I haven't told anyone."

"I hope not, Craig."

"Promise, cross my heart, hope to ..." The rest of the phrase drifted away on Craig's lips. "I didn't hurt her. But I saw you coming out of Val's house. You and that other man."

"Who would they believe anyway?"

"What do you mean, officer?"

"Should you speak about what you saw. Would they listen to me, a policeman? Or you?"

"Nobody hears anything I say." Craig spoke in a quiet voice.

"At the moment, Craig, you're our prime suspect."

Tears welled in Craig's eyes. He wiped them away. "I wouldn't hurt Val, she was my friend."

"So you say, but the evidence tells us otherwise," Carslake softened his voice, as if trying to engage a toddler. "I can help you though."

"What do you mean?"

"There's something I need you to say, when you're asked. And you have to be certain when you say it."

"Say what?"

"That you saw Duncan Usher coming out of Val's house. Duncan Usher. Not me."

"But, that's a lie!"

"Only you and I will know."

"Mum says I should always tell the truth."

"It's either that or prison, Craig." Carslake was starting to get agitated. Time was getting short, he could feel it. "What would happen to your mother if you went to prison?"

"She'd be very upset."

"Mr Usher is a bad man, take it from me. He deserves to go to prison."

"He's always been good to me."

"Do you deserve to go to prison, Craig?"

"I'm not sure."

Carslake could scream. "No. You don't. Now tell me, who did you see coming out of the house?"

Craig thought for a long moment. He cast his eyes downward and eventually muttered, "Mr Usher."

Carslake leaned on the bedstead for support, he was so relieved. "Well done, Craig. Don't speak about this for now. Keep it to yourself, okay?"

"Okay."

"I've got to go."

"Bye."

"Get some sleep."

Carslake slipped out, and not a moment too soon because within half a minute James was back. He'd done it, he'd persuaded Craig, the simpleton. All the lad had to do now was speak up at the right time.

Twenty Two

Then

    When Gray returned to Craig's room he found Molly had gone. James was leaning against the wall, looking out the window at a view of the car park. Craig was in bed, asleep. James turned to face Gray.

"Where's Molly?"

"Gone out for a walk to clear her head and calm down. What do you want?"

Gray raised the DNA test kit. "I'm to take a swab from Craig. For analysis against our findings from the crime scene. Has he eaten or drunk anything in the last hour?"

"No, and I'm not sure I can give you permission. I'm not his dad."

"Molly just did, in the corridor."

"Oh."

"You didn't get the chance to say much earlier."

"As I said, I'm not Craig's dad, so I don't blame Molly for taking control of the conversation."

"Would you consider him capable of hurting Valerie?"

"There's no way. He'd rather have hurt himself."

"It appears he did hurt himself though."

James shook his head. "He's a good kid. Great to spend time with. It's just not everybody gets him."

"So what do you think happened?"

147

James sighed. "I've really no idea. Molly and I have talked about it incessantly over the last few hours. Our only thought was Craig was trying to protect Val. But it's all speculation."

The door opened. Molly entered closing the door behind her.

"DC Gray is here to take a swab from Craig," said James.

"I know," said Molly. "Go ahead, Constable. Let me wake him up, though."

Gray stood back while Molly shook Craig's shoulder. He stirred, groggy, presumably from the drugs.

"Craig, darling. The policeman would like to take a sample from your mouth. Is that okay? Show him, Constable."

Gray held up the swab, a broad cotton tip on a stick, in its packet.

"All right," said Craig wearily.

Gray pulled on a pair nitrile gloves which came in the kit before he tore the packaging. "Open up please, Craig."

Gray rubbed the swab around the inside of Craig's cheek before putting it into a plastic vial and screwing the top on.

"You can close your jaw now," said Molly. Craig did so. He shut his eyes and nodded off to sleep again. "Is that everything you need?"

"Yes, and thank you again."

"No problem, I'll walk you out."

"There's no need."

"I insist."

In the corridor Molly was stopped by a nurse, petite and with dark skin. "How is everything?" she asked, touching Molly on the arm.

"Fine thanks, Bridget." Molly nodded towards Gray. "I'm just with the police right now."

"Oh, sorry. I'll see you later." The nurse walked away without a glance at Gray.

"I'm getting a coffee from the machine," said Molly, "do you want anything?"

"I've had plenty, thanks," said Gray.

Molly led him to a small waiting area off the corridor. Gray waited while she fed coins into the machine, wondering what she had to say away from James. When she had the cup, Molly pointed to a chair. Gray sat. She took a place opposite.

"Craig, he has a few behavioural issues."

"Like what?"

"He's not the fastest learner." Molly frowned. "I had difficulties giving birth. His brain was starved of oxygen for too long. He's a lovely lad, but he's a bit slow and sometimes he doesn't interact well with people."

"How so?"

"He doesn't always understand how to respect boundaries."

"Your husband said he was tactile."

"It's not been easy raising Craig, you know?"

"I can imagine."

"Do you have children?"

"Yes. A boy and a girl."

"Are both healthy?"

"Thankfully, yes."

"Then you can only half get it. Craig's father left soon after he was born. I spent years on my own dealing with all the challenges until James came along. I know people see the age gap, wonder why we're together, but we get along great. That's what matters." She had a sip of the drink. "I'm sorry Valerie's dead, but I'm glad too. Is that a terrible thing?"

"It's not unusual."

"I hated James working there, but we need the money. I'm a nurse here, and it's not a well-paying job, unfortunately."

"Why was it a problem that James was working at Valerie's?"

"Because of her. Valerie. She was always on the lookout for a new man, an escape from her husband. She was a few years ahead of me at school. She was the same back then. A gold digger. Difficult when you live in Thanet. Not a lot glitters on the island."

"Was she interested in James?"

A look of irritation passed across Molly's face. "I don't know for sure. James says no, but I'm not certain. I mean, he's a handsome man, so who could blame her?" She paused. "And who could blame him for wanting Valerie over me?"

"I don't know, Mrs Mundby."

"I've spent my life fighting, Constable Gray. But keeping James from her has been the toughest fight of them all." She put the cup down, closed her eyes, and nodded to herself as if she'd made a decision. "I think you need to take a swab from my husband too."

GRAY PARKED AT THE back of the station, shoving the car in a tight space everyone else had avoided. Carslake was out as soon as the vehicle stopped, squeezing through the gap, striding into the building, report under his arm, Gray in his wake.

"About bloody time," said Copeland when the pair entered one of the meeting spaces off the Major Incident Room. It was just the three of them. The DI liked his meetings to be circumspect; no regular, large gatherings for him unless they were worthwhile. His juniors were responsible for cascading the actions and news down through the ranks. Copeland reckoned it kept minds focused on the case, particularly his own.

This was Gray's first intimate briefing with the big man himself. He was well aware it wasn't a reflection of enhanced status. Simply that he'd been first responder. Which meant Copeland couldn't jettison him.

Copeland took the report from Carslake, pointed towards the seats on the other side of the table. Gray waited for his inspector to finish; irritated with being made to sit here when he had plenty to get on with. Copeland separated the photos and spread them out across the surface. He took his time staring at one image after another. Gray noticed Carslake looking everywhere but the table.

Finally Copeland spoke.

"I should tell you two the latest," he said. "Brazier has done some good work for once. He said the bedroom was spotless. Vacuumed and wiped down, so there's virtually no trace evidence available for analysis."

"Jenkinson said Mrs Usher's corpse was pristine too."

"Meaning Craig Mundby strangled Valerie, then cleaned up before he tried to kill himself," said Carslake.

"That's one explanation." Copeland picked up the report again. "There's several scenarios. Either, as you say, Craig killed her, then stuck around before slashing his wrists. Or Valerie was murdered, and the killer dressed the scene up as a murder suicide."

"Why would he do that? It makes no sense," said Gray.

"Remorse, perhaps?" said Carslake.

"We need to know who had sex with Valerie before she died," said Copeland. "That's the key. And have you been to the security company yet, Sol? I want the CCTV footage from the camera outside Valerie's house."

"Not yet, sir."

"What are you waiting for? Get going!"

Twenty Three

N^{ow} As Gray left Copeland's house, Usher covered his face up with a hand in case Gray glanced in his direction. He didn't. Gray just headed back to where he was staying for the night. Telfer had parked in the opposite direction, assuming correctly that Gray was unlikely to head in the more rural direction.

Earlier, Usher had watched Gray enter Copeland's place. He'd dealt with the intervening time watching the small world of Wetheral go about its business. He was used to long stretches of time with nothing happening. The only event of interest was when Copeland's wife exited. She drove away in a smart 4x4 Mercedes.

"What now?" asked Telfer. "Go and see him?"

"We keep waiting."

"How long?"

Usher didn't reply, there was no need. Copeland, dressed in wellington boots, wax jacket, and flat cap, withdrew. Two dogs shot past him. He pulled the door to, then got walking, swinging a cane with every other stride. Copeland navigated the road and crossed the green.

"Wait here," said Usher before sliding out. He followed Copeland, remaining a few hundred yards behind. The path turned into a muddy trail which ran beside a river. Usher paid no heed to the mire; he'd be dumping everything he wore when it was done anyway.

After a few minutes, the path emerged from the greenery. Just ahead were the yellow-brick arches of Corby Bridge, a Victorian viaduct which stretched across the river. Usher paused. Copeland was just standing there, staring at the river. The dogs gambolled about, ignored by their master. Glancing up and down the path to ensure they were alone, Usher decided here was as good as anywhere.

Copeland wasn't aware of Usher's approach until they were standing side by side. The irritated expression on his face dropped as soon as he recognised the man beside him.

"Nice chat with Sergeant Gray?" asked Usher.

"What do you want?"

To Usher's disappointment Copeland stumbled over his words.

"Where's the big man I once knew?" he mocked the retired policeman.

Spurred into sudden action, Copeland made his way past Usher. But he didn't get far. Usher grabbed his arm, his grip not allowing him to proceed.

"What do you want?" repeated Copeland.

"Did you kill her?"

"It wasn't me!"

Usher stared deep into Copeland's eyes as he had done with many others in the past, when he was beating confessions out of men who'd crossed him. He believed Copeland.

"Was it Gray?"

"Let me go." Copeland tried and failed to shake off Usher's grip.

"I don't think so." Usher back handed Copeland, who staggered backwards a few steps with the blow. Copeland put fingers to his lips, came away with blood. Copeland ran but Usher was faster and was on him within twenty yards. Usher barrelled into Copeland's back, knocking him sprawling onto the hard ground, his cane spinning away. Usher heard the breath explode out of Copeland's lungs. Usher leaned down, grabbed a bunch of the old man's clothes and began to drag him towards the river. Copeland struggled, flailing at Usher.

"Help! Help me!" shouted Copeland, but there was nobody around to hear him.

Usher stepped into the river, ignoring the cold bite of the current as it coursed around and through his legs. Copeland began to buck and heave but Usher dragged him out further, until the water was around his thighs. In desperation, Copeland bit down on Usher's restraining hand, but Usher grabbed Copeland's ear and twisted hard until he screamed. Usher forced Copeland's head under water. Copeland thrashed, but Usher was much stronger. Eventually, the thrashing lessened. It took less than a minute before Copeland went limp. Usher held him beneath the surface for a while longer before he let go. Copeland floated away, face down.

Usher walked back up onto the bank, his chest heaving with the effort and the adrenalin. He picked up Copeland's walking cane and tossed it into the water. The dogs whined and shook their tails, uncertain of what had just occurred. Usher patted one on the head and walked back towards the car. Someone would find Copeland's corpse soon.

Twenty Four

T^{hen} Gray paused outside the offices of Raptor Security in Ramsgate. The logo was a side shot of a dinosaur; a T-Rex with the strapline, "Our protection bites". It reminded Gray of the film *Jurassic Park*. Thanet was about as far away culturally as you could get from Hollywood.

Raptor was located on a narrow back street near the Royal Harbour, one of those strange arrangements where terraced residential houses nestled up, cheek by jowl, against commercial ventures. Double yellows stretched all along the street. Even a badly positioned bicycle would block the road. There was limited parking adjacent to the building. A van with Raptor livery on the side pulled out, leaving a space for Gray.

An alarm beeped when Gray opened the door and stepped inside. The reception area was a small hallway painted white and brightly lit thanks to a large window which occupied most of the front wall. A set of stairs ran upwards, beneath which was a table and chairs. A door next to the stairs opened and a young Indian woman wearing a short skirt stepped out.

"Can I help?" she asked.

Gray showed his warrant card. "I'm here to see the owner."

"Nathan? I'll just see if he's available. What's it regarding please?"

"One of his installations."

"I'll be right back."

But she wasn't. Gray waited for a good ten minutes before someone descended the stairs. Halfway down, a man with a shiny bald head and a bushy beard paused, bending over so he could see into the reception area.

"Sergeant Gray? I'm Nathan Wade. Do you want to come up?"

Gray followed Wade up the stairs. Wade said, "Get this weather, it's crazy for the time of year, isn't it?"

"I haven't really been paying attention."

Wade, who was a good foot taller than Gray, had paused at the top and held open the door. "Too busy catching crooks? Ha ha."

"If you like, sir."

The smile slipped from Wade's face. Gray passed Wade and entered his office, which possessed a view over the street through expansive windows. The house opposite felt close enough to lean across and touch. There was a pale wooden desk – its surface empty except for a laptop – and a leather recliner opposite the desk. Beyond were a couple of chairs around a table which Wade directed Gray to. On the walls were large photos on stretched canvas of various tourist spots from Thanet.

"Take a seat, please. I'm sorry I kept you. Somebody wouldn't get off the phone. I understand there's a problem with one of my alarms?"

"Not as such," said Gray. "I'm after some information about the security at a property on Castle Avenue."

"Okay. Let me take a look." Wade collected his laptop and placed it on the table. "What's the house number?"

Gray told him.

"Duncan Usher," said Wade, not needing to drag the data out of his system. He sat back. "I did this one myself. Our top-of-the-range products throughout; monitored alarm, individual key codes, CCTV, the works."

"Not Mrs Usher?"

"No, it was Duncan who commissioned the work. I've known him quite a while."

"You mentioned a monitored alarm, if someone trips it who gets notified?"

"Raptor does. We've got twenty-four-hour cover. When we get an alert, we contact the customer. If there's no answer, we call the police immediately. There's a running log of every activity at the property when it comes to the security elements. I can access the information right now on my laptop, if you like."

"Please. For Saturday in particular."

Wade tapped away at the keys before spinning it around so the screen faced Gray.

"What am I looking at?" asked Gray.

Wade moved beside Gray's shoulder. He bent over and pointed at a line. "See here, this tells me if the alarm is switched on or off, whether it's the whole house inside and outside, if the occupant is out for the day, or just the external sensors for when people are inside but want to be aware if somebody is breaking in. There's a panic alarm by the bed too."

Gray hadn't been aware of that.

"I can tell you," said Wade, "that the alarm was switched off the entire day. The gates were closed, but later opened and remained so from just after 8 p.m."

"The key codes, who sets those?"

Wade returned to his seat. "They're supplied with a factory number which is 0000. The client changes them at installation."

"So you don't know what they are?"

"No."

"What if there's a problem, and you need to gain access?"

"There's an override code. There has to be."

"Is it only you who has the code?"

"Usually, yes."

"Not always?"

Wade shifted uncomfortably in his seat. "No."

"Did you give Duncan Usher the override?"

"It's not illegal to do so."

"Answer the question, please."

"He wanted it."

"So Duncan Usher could walk into the house at any time he pleased?"

"Yes."

Twenty Five

N**ow** Gray woke feeling groggy. He checked his watch, surprised to see an hour and a half had passed. He'd only meant to get five minutes' rest. Copeland would more than likely be waiting for him. Gray headed downstairs. He wandered through the bar but didn't see Copeland. He sat at a small table and ordered a coffee to rouse himself.

A previous occupant had left behind a copy of the day's newspaper. A red top which Gray wouldn't normally read. Gray flicked through it, ignoring the insalubrious stories about so-called celebrities and racier, politically biased narratives. A blurb about Usher's release was on page five. He was already becoming yesterday's news.

Gray finished the coffee long after the paper. He checked his watch, debating whether to wait or go find Copeland. His impatience won out. After collecting his coat from his room, he walked the short distance back to the centre of Wetheral. When he rounded the corner he stopped in surprise. Two police cars were parked outside Copeland's house, bracing the driveway. There were a couple of uniforms and two others, a man and a woman, who were clearly CID talking to a handful of locals. Gray headed over to the edge of the group.

"What's going on?" asked Gray of an old man who had more hair sticking out of his nose and ears than on his head.

"Terry's been found dead," he said.

"How?"

"Drowned, I hear." The old man crossed himself.

Gray saw movement in an upper window, a smear of pale in the dark backdrop, peering out. Then she was gone. Sarah. She would have told the police about him. Gray made his way over to one of the officers.

"DS Draycott," she said by way of introduction.

"DS Gray, Kent police." He handed over his warrant card.

Draycott eyed Gray. "Bit off your patch?"

Gray repeated the story about being on holiday for a few days and coming to see an old colleague. Draycott waved her boss over.

DI Mather examined Gray's warrant card too, passed it back and shook Gray's hand. "So you were with Chief Superintendent Copeland earlier?" he asked.

"Yes. When I left him, he was going for a walk with the dogs."

"What time was this?"

"A couple of hours ago. We were due to meet in The Crown, but he never turned up. I became concerned and came over."

"How was he?"

"Fine, as far as I could tell. It's been a few years since we last met, though. What happened? Someone said he drowned."

"Looks that way. Maybe he slipped and fell in, banged his head. We'll know more from the autopsy."

"No witnesses?"

"None."

"How's his wife?"

"As to be expected," said Draycott. "In shock. All's fine when she goes out. Finds out her husband's dead on her return."

"Did you work for DCI Copeland too?" asked Gray.

Both Draycott and Mather nodded.

"How long are you planning to stay?" asked Mather.

"I'm leaving tomorrow. Unless you need me here longer?"

"I wouldn't think so. Give me your number so I can get in touch if I have to."

Gray passed on his details, then left the scene wondering what had really happened to Copeland.

Twenty Six

Then
    Gray pulled up near his house, a tall terrace on a quiet street in Broadstairs. As it was after 5 p.m., he wasn't able to park directly outside. The properties had been built before the First World War, so off-street parking was rare and on-street parking was a premium.

Bloody Copeland. Gray still wasn't convinced Usher was actually guilty, despite how his DI was making the evidence line up. The evidence was circumstantial and there were too many unanswered questions. Though he had to admit the information he'd just gleaned from Raptor was pretty damning. He tried to shake off the tiredness. He could do with a drink. Gray dug out his phone and called Carslake, telling him what Wade had said.

"Usher has the code?" asked Carslake.

"Apparently so."

"Fantastic information, Sol, well done."

"No problem."

Gray jumped when someone banged on his window. It was Hope, waving at him, a big grin on her face. She was wearing blue pyjamas. No pink for her.

"Sol, are you still there?"

"Yes, sorry."

"Is there anything else?"

"That's all." Hope was tugging on the door handle.

"Okay, get some rest. And well done again." Carslake disconnected as Hope yanked his door open, leaning backwards to make the heavy weight swing on its hinges. Gray pulled the keys out of the ignition and stepped onto the pavement.

"Daddy!" Hope buried herself into his legs. He picked her up and held her to him. She sank her head onto his shoulder, long curly hair covering her face. "I missed you, Daddy."

"I missed you too, darling."

Gray walked back the short distance to his house carrying her.

Kate was standing in the doorway, balancing Tom on her hip. She was as beautiful as ever, despite the stresses and strain on her mind and body of having two young children. Kate's hair was going grey already even though she was only twenty-nine, a year younger than Gray. She used to dye it, though now she was letting the natural colour come through. Kate hated it, but Gray didn't care.

"I kept them up until you came home," said Kate. "They've been desperate to see you."

"Me too."

Their son, Tom, only eighteen months old, was about walking and his teeth were through. Kate was struggling to hold him as he stretched out for his father waving, grinning. Gray took him in his spare arm, then bent to kiss Kate on the forehead. Together they went inside, and Kate closed the door.

Gray sighed inside when Alice Newbold, Kate's friend from church, entered the corridor from the kitchen. She was a small woman, with a hairstyle that hadn't changed for years – a loose perm held in place come rain or shine by a large volume of sticky hairspray. Alice was regularly teasing her hair with the pointed end of a comb, coaxing a few strands back into place and freezing them with more spray.

When Gray was busy with work, Kate tended to lean on Alice. She was retired and spent most of her time either at the church or with the parishioners. Since Tom's birth, Kate had become a bit of a mission for her. It irritated Gray that Alice had the run of the house, but he stayed quiet because he knew how important Alice was to Kate.

"Hello, Sol."

"Alice."

"Now you're home at last. I'll leave you two alone. Art will be agitating for his dinner." Alice touched Kate on the arm. "Remember what we discussed."

"I will and thanks Alice, see you soon."

"It's no problem at all." Alice kissed Hope on the cheek, eliciting a grimace.

Good girl, thought Gray.

Tom accepted a ruffling of his hair with limited grace.

"God bless you both." Alice left, the door clicking shut behind her.

"Come on, let's get you up to bed," said Kate.

"Mummy!" shouted Hope, her bottom lip out in a pout. She was already exhibiting a wilful and independent character. Something Gray wanted, but didn't. Not until they were old enough to fend for themselves, at least.

"I'll read you a story," said Gray.

"Not the gingerbread man again!" said Hope as they climbed the stairs. It was Tom's favourite. "He's heard it a thousand times."

"You can have something else instead. What would you like?"

"I've an idea."

"Let me read to Tom, and then I'll come into you."

Gray lay Tom down in his cot; he was on the verge of needing a bed. At least he was in his own room now, giving Gray and Kate some privacy and personal time. A Moses basket at the bottom of the bed with a wailing child in it was a real passion killer.

Tom listened with rapt attention to his favourite story, Gray snapping the book shut at the end like the crocodile closing his jaws. Tom wanted to hear the story all over again.

"It's time to get some sleep, son," said Gray. He pulled the door to, just enough to allow a sliver of light from the landing to fall inside. Hope was sitting up in bed.

"Finally," she said and handed Gray a book. Mister Bump. Gray read to Hope. She giggled all the way through.

She loved words. If she'd been naughty, the major punishment was to withdraw stories.

"Can you read it again, please?" asked Hope at the end.

"No, darling. You need to get some sleep for school tomorrow."

Hope enjoyed her lessons. So different from his day when going to school was a case of survival of the fittest, show no fear, take the bullying. Everything was more pastoral now. Gray kissed Hope on the forehead.

She lay down. "I don't want the duvet, it's too hot."

"Okay. It's there if you want it."

"Night, Daddy."

"Night, Princess."

"Love you loads."

"Love you more."

Gray closed her door. Compared to Tom she preferred darkness. Gray always marvelled at how two children, from the same parents and raised in the same way, could be so different.

Kate was waiting for Gray in the kitchen with a glass of red wine. She handed it over and he drank most of it in one swig.

Gray topped up his glass and zoned out for a moment.

"It'll never happen to us," said Kate, recognising Gray's deepest fears because he'd expressed them to her several times before.

"I hope not."

"It won't. Do you know why?"

"You're going to tell me, I'm sure."

Kate scowled. "Because we have you, Solomon Gray. You're our protector."

She stepped inside Gray's arms and he gave her a tight hug.

Eventually he asked, "What were you and Alice talking about?"

"When?"

"Earlier, Alice said to remember what you'd discussed."

"Oh, it was nothing, just Alice wanting me help at the church more, to get me out of the house."

Gray poured himself more wine.

"Tough day?" asked Kate.

"Tough few days."

The night that Valerie Usher had been murdered, Gray had come home and stood in the doorway of Hope's room, staring at her as she slept. Kate found him. He'd no idea how long she'd been there. He told Kate then about the Usher case, to explain why she'd see little of him for a while.

"That boss of yours – Copeland. He works everyone in his team to the bone. Why? Not for *you*."

"He's not too bad, Kate."

"Who do you think listens to you every day? You're constantly bitching about the man."

Gray topped up his glass. He felt Kate's eyes watching his every move.

"Do I?"

"Yes!"

"Have you been talking to Alice about him?"

Kate glanced down at her feet. "Maybe."

"I don't like you discussing private matters with Alice. It's got nothing to do with her."

"She's my friend."

"I know, but some things that should stay just between us."

"So why is it I feel I can speak to Alice when I can't to you, Sol?"

"You can talk to me about anything."

"Can I? You're at work all the time, and on the rare occasions you're home you're shattered. Look at you now, you can barely stand. And you're drinking a lot more. The bottle's half gone already. It's since you made the move to CID."

"I worked long and hard for that."

"I know. Me and the children have sacrificed a lot too."

"It'll get better."

"Will it?"

"One day."

"When?"

"Soon."

"I miss you, Sol. The kids need their daddy." Kate looked him in the eyes, a pleading expression on her face. "I'd like you to change jobs."

Gray couldn't believe what he was hearing. "Leave CID?"

"Leave the police."

"We've been through this."

"Not really. I mentioned it, and you said no. That's not really a discussion."

"The police is all I know. What else would I do?"

"I don't know," her voice was wavering. "At least we'd have our family in one piece!"

"We'll always have our family, Kate," he pulled her close.

"Will we? Sometimes I wonder."

"Daddy?" Hope was standing in the doorway, rubbing her eyes. "I heard you shouting."

"Me and Mummy are just having a conversation. Let's get you back to bed."

Gray carried Hope upstairs. It took a few minutes to settle her. Kate was gone when he returned downstairs. He went back up a few steps and saw their bedroom door firmly closed. Gray guessed he'd be sleeping downstairs tonight.

Twenty Seven

Now Gray caught an early morning train back to Thanet. His sleep had been restless, fragments of his last conversation with Copeland played through his head. All the way home, as the countryside whizzed by his window, the manner of Copeland's demise stayed on his mind. It was afternoon by the time he stepped off the train, and the day was pleasantly warm.

Back at his flat, Gray headed out onto the balcony along with his mobile and the letter he'd received from the hospital a few days ago regarding his upcoming treatment. He dialled the number at the top of the page.

"Doctor Manesh? It's Solomon Gray."

"Ah, Mr Gray, good to hear from you," said Manesh. Gray knew he was a Sri Lankan by birth. From Kandy. Finest tea on the planet, apparently. Doctor Manesh liked to talk.

"I got your letter about my next appointment."

"Yes, it is going well, Mr Gray. A few more, and we should have you in remission."

"I'm afraid there's a problem."

"Oh?"

"I've got a challenging case at the moment, so I have to delay the treatment."

"No, no Mr Gray, you must not do that."

"It won't be for long, a few weeks at the most."

"I would urge you to complete the course at the earliest opportunity."

"I can't doctor. I'm needed."

"Then your supervisor has to find somebody else."

"That's impossible. I'm personally critical to the investigation."

Dr Manesh sighed heavily. "Well, I can't force you to have the treatment, but I recommend, in the strongest possible terms Mr Gray, not to delay the process. It is likely to set back your advancement and may ultimately mean we can't successfully destroy your cancer."

"So it's potentially a life or death decision?"

"That is one way of looking at it, yes."

Gray considered Dr Manesh's words. They had no impact on his choice. "Thank you for your advice, but I have to do this. I'll be back in touch as quickly as I can."

"The sooner the better. Goodbye, Mr Gray."

Gray disconnected. He hoped so, too. His mobile rang almost immediately.

It was Fowler. "I can hear seagulls, are you sunning yourself?" he asked. The humour sounded forced to Gray.

"Inside, outside, makes no difference they're so loud. What's up, Mike?"

"I need to have a chat. I know you're on holiday again, but is it okay if I pop round?"

"Of course."

"Over a beer? I could really do with one."

Gray checked his watch, barely after 2 p.m. "It's a bit early."

"Not for me. See you in the Albion. Twenty minutes all right?"

"Sure." Gray cut the call. Fowler had seemed even gloomier than usual.

It was a ten-minute saunter for Gray to reach the Albion Hotel, a clifftop establishment boasting spectacular views. On a clear day like today, the horizon was a stretch of blue sky and sea. Once owned by the same family for a century, they'd sold out to a major brewery a few years ago. No heirs interested in taking on the business, apparently.

Gray went inside, managed to bag a table by the window, and ordered himself a sparkling mineral water while he awaited Fowler. He got halfway down by the time Fowler arrived, late.

"Parking is a bloody nightmare around here," he said, shaking his head. His shirt was open at the neck, his tie loosened.

"At least the summer holiday season is done. A few weeks ago you wouldn't have found a space within a mile."

Fowler pointed at Gray's glass. "What's that, water?"

"What's wrong with water?"

"What's right with it? Wait," Fowler put a hand over his heart and staggered theatrically. "Are you ill? Shall I call an ambulance? Must be bad if you're on that stuff."

"Very funny. I'm just a bit dehydrated is all."

"Do you want a proper drink then?"

"I'm fine with this, thanks."

Gray watched Fowler while he was waiting at the bar. He looked scruffier than usual, his suit wrinkled, hair ruffled. Fowler obviously wanted to ask how it had gone with the IPCC. Gray could read him like a book.

Fowler soon returned with two pints of Guinness, he sat down, took a deep gulp from the glass. Gray noticed the area under Fowler's eyes was black.

"Water, what's the point?" asked Fowler.

"Not getting fired for drinking on the job?"

Fowler shrugged.

"I said I didn't want a beer."

"They're both for me." Fowler said it as if his statement should be obvious and Gray was stupid for asking.

"What's going on, Mike?"

"Nothing."

"Bullshit. You're downing the booze while on shift, and you look like you've run through a hedge several times."

Fowler shrugged again and started on his second pint.

"How's Yvonne?" asked Gray.

"At work or home?"

"Both."

"Crabby and crabbier." Fowler pulled a face like he'd smelt something gone off. "Ever since we moved in together." He gave a deep sigh.

"What?"

"She has... expectations, I guess. On how we should live. Suddenly there's flowers and cushions everywhere."

"That's it? Home decor?"

Fowler raised his hands. "I don't know, it's just ..." He dropped his hands again. "She's always watching me, measuring me. Nothing I do is good enough, I don't know." Fowler sank the rest of his pint in one go then wiped his top lip clear of foam. "Can we change the subject?"

"It was you who said you wanted to talk."

"Yes, but about the Lone Ranger and Tonto, not Hamson."

"Who?"

"Smits and Wyatt?"

"I don't understand."

"A pair of cowboys, get it?"

Gray didn't bother pointing out one was a Native American and so quite the opposite of a cowboy.

"I'm getting another beer, one for you too?" asked Fowler.

"Lime and soda."

"Bloody hell, Sol. You're becoming an embarrassment to be seen out in public with." Fowler headed to the bar, leaving Gray to ponder what might have been said by the cowboys, as Fowler put it, to make him so keen to speak with Gray. And so eager to drink it away.

When Fowler returned, glasses in hand, he sat down, took a gulp of his pint. He pondered Gray for a moment before saying, "I've had an interview but got told straight away they weren't interested in me as I was just a lowly PC at the time. I'd been standing on the wrong side of the cordon. So there was little I could have done to influence events. Very nice of Smits to say so."

"It was over quickly then."

"You'd think so, but no. Smits went on for ages. The majority of his questions focused on you," Fowler raised his glass in salute. "Asking where you were at certain points in the case, what you investigated, who you spoke to. Stuff like that. I couldn't tell him a great deal."

"Couldn't or wouldn't?"

"Both, mate. I don't like Smits. There's something about him I can't put my finger on."

"Did they ask about Carslake or Copeland?"

"Barely. It was all Gray, Gray, Gray, and more Gray. It was weird. If I was just a lowly PC back then, why ask all these questions about you, a lowly DC? Why not Copeland or even Carslake?"

"No idea."

"Copeland, turning up dead, though. And drowned too. He always made out it'd be in his bed at a ripe old age."

"Comes to us all eventually. Thanks for the heads up, by the way."

The pair fell silent for a few minutes, each with their own thoughts. Gray had an image of the two of them sitting in a pub when they were long retired, just like this. Reminiscing over old cases, old rivalries, punctured by long pauses.

"I'd better get back to the station," said Fowler. "Make sure Yvonne sees me grafting."

"You're like an old married couple, you two." They'd been seeing each other a couple of years.

Fowler took a long drink, put the glass down slowly and stared at it while he wiped some condensation away. "Actually, I think we might be over."

"Can't you work at it?"

"I don't know how."

Gray had nothing he could say to make Fowler's situation better. If Fowler wanted a relationship counsellor, Gray was the last person he should be choosing. "I'm sorry to hear that, really, I am."

"Thanks."

"Look, Mike, if you ever need anything, just ask."

"Really?"

"Of course. How long have we known each other?"

Fowler nodded. He appeared about to say something, but he got up without a word, drained what was left in his glass and left Gray alone at the table.

Gray stared out at the sea. Perhaps a couple of sentences here about him ruminating over Copeland's death and how he finds it odd that Smits and the Wyatt didn't seem to be focusing on the case's two lead investigators, Copeland and Carslake.

His phone jolted him back to reality. He didn't recognise the number. "Hello?"

"DS Gray, it's Eric Smits. Can you talk?"

Gray refrained from telling Smits it was a stupid question, they already were.

"Yes."

"Good, I understand you're returning to work tomorrow?"

"I only booked two days off so, yes, I'll be in."

"I'd like to have a meeting with you. I've a few more questions."

"What about?"

"We can get into that tomorrow. How does 8 a.m. sound? Before you get sucked back into the day-to-day?"

"I can do that."

"Good, I look forward to talking, Sergeant Gray."

Twenty Eight

T**hen**

The ringing of the mobile woke Gray from an uncomfortable sleep. He groaned, an ache in his back making him wince. His head hurt too, but from the wine, rather than the angle of his posture. He flicked on the lamp, pushed back the cover and groped for the phone.

"Sol, it's Jeff. Sorry to wake you so early. We've had a development."

"What?"

"I'll explain in the car. Be ready in ten minutes, I'm picking you up."

Gray grabbed a quick shower before creeping into the bedroom to get some fresh clothes. Carslake was already outside waiting when Gray stepped outside. It felt fresher, like the weather was beginning to turn at last and autumn was properly on the way.

The car was moving again before Gray had his seatbelt on. The clock on the dash said 6:13 a.m. Gray was glad to be out of the house before Kate was up and about. He wasn't sure he was ready to talk after her demands of last night.

"What's going on, Jeff?"

"Feedback from the door-to-door has come in. Someone was seen hanging around Mrs Usher's house over recent weeks.

Craig Mundby. We're going to the hospital to interview him and Molly."

MOLLY MUNDBY WAS IN the room with Craig. There was a cot set up next to his bed. The covers were turned back, the bottom sheet wrinkled, and a head-shaped dent in the pillow. Molly was sitting in the same chair as yesterday, wearing a yellow bathrobe, bunny slippers on her feet, and holding a plastic cup. Craig was out of it, unconscious with drugs or simply asleep. Gray didn't know.

"Where's your husband?" asked Carslake.

"Not here, clearly," said Molly. She had dark circles under her eyes, and her hair was a mess. "Probably at home." She sighed, rubbed one eye. "What do you want now?"

"To ask a few more questions."

"At this time of the morning?"

"I'm sorry, yes. We'll be as quick as we can."

Molly huffed. "Okay."

"Thank you. We've been conducting a door-to-door in the area following Mrs Usher's murder. Some information which may be of value has come to light."

"What's this got to do with us?"

"Several witnesses stated that they've seen Craig hanging around outside Mrs Usher's house on several occasions over recent weeks."

Molly didn't respond immediately. Gray said, "Mrs Mundby?"

She sagged and said, "It's not what you think. The neighbours know that if they see him standing around to tell me or James. We come and get him. I'm surprised you weren't told."

"It's different when there's a policeman on your doorstep asking questions, Mrs Mundby," said Carslake. "From our records it's clear nobody has ever reported this to the police."

"Why would they? He doesn't do any harm."

"Was Mrs Usher aware of Craig's behaviour?"

"I don't know. We weren't exactly the best of friends."

"Why didn't you tell us this yesterday?" asked Gray.

"I didn't think it pertinent. Craig's harmless."

"If there's anything else you want to say, now's the time," said Carslake.

Molly stood up, as if she'd made a decision. "There is, but you should hear it from Craig." Molly woke her son up in the same manner as the day before, gently stroking his face until he stirred. Craig blinked, taking in Gray and Carslake's presence as if it were entirely normal.

"Darling," said Molly, "do you remember the conversation we had last night after these policemen left?" Craig's eyes flicked between Gray and Carslake. He nodded. "Can you repeat what you told me?" Another nod.

"I was standing outside Valerie's house the night she—" Craig sniffed, unable to speak the words. "I saw movement at the front door. It was Duncan. He came out and told me Valerie was in trouble and needed my help." Craig paused again, the memory seemingly causing him some trouble.

"Go on, Craig," said Carslake.

"I went inside with him, and the next thing I remembered was waking up in here." Craig sniffed. "Why would Duncan attack me? I thought he was my friend."

"DO YOU BELIEVE THE pair of them?" asked Carslake. He was in the passenger seat this time; Gray the driver. He'd had to ratchet the seat forward a couple of notches as Carslake's bearing was more laid back than Gray's.

"She seemed genuine," said Gray. "But Molly separately admitted to me she didn't like Valerie. There's clearly tension between her and James on the subject. And Craig is her son. She's spent her life defending him."

"You know what Copeland is going to make of this?"

"Another nail in Usher's coffin."

"Yes, and Copeland wielding the hammer. Means, motive, and opportunity, Sol. Usher has them all."

At the station they found Copeland in the Major Incident Room, staring at the murder board, filled with notes and photos on Valerie and Duncan Usher and Craig Mundby. "What did the lad have to say for himself?"

Carslake repeated their conversation.

Copeland raised his eyebrows when Carslake told him Craig claimed to have been beckoned in by Usher. "Interesting. We've got the report on the organic material Jenkinson found underneath Valerie's nails. Analysis on the swabs you took of Craig and James yesterday, Sol also came back negative. We got one hit, though." Copeland paused, enjoying the moment. "Duncan Usher. We've got the bastard."

Twenty Nine

N^{ow} *Another restless night.* Gray woke early. The upcoming interview with Smits had played on his mind and disturbed his sleep. He took a shower, dressed, and headed into work. When he arrived, the station was quiet. The night shift was still a couple of hours from finishing. Gray made himself a coffee. He'd need a steady drip of caffeine throughout the day, he reckoned.

He sifted through the emails which had built up while he was out. A couple of minutes before 8 a.m., he made a fresh brew, leaving a cup on Fowler's desk for when he came in, then headed upstairs. Wyatt was already seated. She stood and shook Gray's hand.

"Eric will be here in a minute or two. Take a seat, would you?"

Gray seated himself and didn't attempt to fill the silence. It wasn't his style, and it seemed not to be Wyatt's either. Despite the circumstances, he liked her. She had an easy presence. When Smits arrived, he bustled in with an armful of paperwork in one hand, and a plastic cup of coffee in the other.

"Sorry I'm late." He put everything down on the table before shutting the door with his foot, then sitting opposite Wyatt so that Gray was bracketed by the pair. Smits went through the process of starting the recorder, detailing the date, time, and who was present. Then he paused, let the seconds stretch.

"Tell us about Duncan Usher, Sergeant Gray. What's he like?"

"I hadn't seen him for fifteen years until he was on the TV a couple of days ago."

"You didn't know Usher back then?"

"Only of him. Until his wife died."

"So there wasn't a personal relationship between the pair of you?"

"Why would there be?"

Smits stared at Gray for a long moment before he brought over the paperwork he'd carried in. He laid a document in front of Gray. "Do you recognise this?"

His heart sank. "It's my report from the night Valerie Usher was found murdered." It was the original document.

"And this?"

"My report from an interview at Raptor Security." Smits laid out several more pieces of paper, Gray affirming his knowledge of them all.

"What's your point?" asked Gray.

"Good question." Smits withdrew the originals and replaced them with copies. There were red marks and circles in multiple locations across the pages. "Did you write this?"

Gray picked up the uppermost document and took his time to read it. "In part," he said, handing it back to Smits. He moved to the next document.

"What does that mean?" asked Smits while Gray skimmed over the words. He made Smits wait.

"I think the document was altered after I submitted it."

"But this is your signature, correct?" Smits tapped the scrawl at the foot of the page.

"Yes."

"Then it's your statement."

"As I said, in part. Somebody changed it."

"Who?"

"I don't know. This is the first time I've seen these since I submitted them," lied Gray.

"So how can you be sure the document was altered?"

"Because I know how to spell."

"Based on this evidence, our supposition is someone deliberately falsified official police paperwork in order to mislead the investigation with the purpose of incriminating Duncan Usher and obtaining a guilty verdict."

"That's a reasonable conclusion to draw. But it wasn't me."

Smits shared a glance with Wyatt. She nodded at him. "Okay, we're done with this for now." Smits switched off the recorder. Gray stood.

"Sit back down please," said Wyatt. Gray did so, wondering what was going on.

"We believe you."

"Why?"

"Terry Copeland had previously been reprimanded for lining up evidence to suit his objective. He was suspended following his last case but retired before disciplinary procedures could be completed. I've seen the prosecutor's conclusions. He would have been found guilty and dismissed from the police had the investigation run its course.

"With Copeland's death we can't, of course, question him again on this matter. Which leaves you in the firing line. Regardless of what really happened, the data I have in front of me points towards collusion as a minimum. Whether you willingly went along with Copeland, or as you claim, records were falsified, remains to be established."

"I had nothing to do with it."

"Speaking of Copeland, you travelled all the way up to Cumbria to see your old boss after such a long time. Why?"

"It wasn't specifically to see Copeland."

"According to local officers, you stayed overnight in a hotel in the same village."

Gray shifted in his seat, easily caught in the subterfuge.

"I can appreciate it's difficult for you to trust us, but I assure you neither Emily nor I are out to get you. Quite the opposite. We need your help."

"With what?"

"The real reason we're here," said Wyatt, leaning forward, "is Jeff Carslake."

"I thought this was an investigation into the Usher case?"

"It is, Solomon. May I call you Solomon by the way?" Gray nodded, his mind on Wyatt's reveal, rather than his new desire to be informal. "But with Carslake at the heart. This is where it started."

Wyatt tapped Gray's amended paperwork. "This is where he began to break the law, rather than uphold it. But Carslake is clever; he's stayed under the radar for years. He only made two mistakes in all that time. One was Duncan Usher. The other, indirectly, was your son."

Gray gripped the edge of the table. "What are you saying? How was he involved with Tom?"

"Have you heard the name Lewis Strang before, Solomon?"

"I want to know about Tom, not this bloody Strang, who-ever he is."

"He's highly pertinent, believe me. Back in the day, Strang was something of a legend in the Manchester police force. He had an amazing clearance rate. He got a promotion, moved south to the Met, and his performance continued. Back in the 90s, the Met Commissioner, Paul Condon, set up a shadow group of detectives, known as the Ghost Squad, to investigate corruption at the Met which was, frankly, rife. Strang came to their attention, but he learned of their interest and scaled back his illegal behaviour."

"What has this got to do with Tom or Carslake?"

"Somehow, we're not sure yet, Carslake came into Strang's orbit. The two worked together on mutually beneficial pro-jects. Strang helped Carslake deal with an inconvenience he was struggling with. You, Solomon."

"Me?"

"You couldn't be bought. And Carslake thought that would be a problem for him one day. He needed something to distract you. And that was Tom's disappearance."

Gray leapt to his feet, ready to storm into Carslake's office. But Smits got to the door first, he was nearer.

"I don't blame you, but this isn't the way," said Smits, block-ing Gray's exit.

"He might know where Tom is."

"And if he does, we'll find out. That's why Emily is here."

"Jesus!" Gray blew out a lungful of air, ran his hands through his hair. He clenched and unclenched his fists, pacing back and forth. Eventually he said, "What do you want me to do?"

"Help bring him down. End his career, put him in prison and anybody else he was working with."

"How?"

Wyatt smiled. "First, we're going to suspend you."

GRAY HARDLY SAW THE waves smash themselves against the concrete curve of the esplanade. The roar of the water was drowned out by the noise in his head as he thought about what Smits had told him. He rested on the railings, head down, seeing nothing.

Gray recalled Hamson's face when Smits had informed her of his suspension, pending further investigation for falsifying records. Her expression had been a mix of disbelief and acceptance. Like she hadn't been totally surprised by Gray's transgression.

Then Smits had asked where Fowler was. Hamson told him Fowler hadn't turned in so far. Gray barely heard a word of their conversation.

As soon as Smits let him go, Gray left the station and headed down the cliff road past the Winter Gardens to stand beside the sea. News of his suspension would be all over the station now. Gray wondered if Carslake would call. He suspected not.

Tom's disappearance was down to his friend. Ex-friend. If he was honest with himself, Gray had suspected Carslake was dirty for a while. Hamson had often told him about her lack of trust in the DCI. Perhaps that's what had made him shut his ears to the accusations even more?

Smits had handed Gray a plan. For now, he just needed to go home and wait for Wyatt to contact him.

Thirty

T**hen**
   The full complement of CID and many of the beat cops were crammed into the Incident Room. All the seats were taken; it was standing room only. Gray sat towards the back, between Carslake and Fowler.

"What's going on?" asked Fowler.

"Just wait, you'll find out," said Gray.

Copeland was front and centre, waiting for silence to fall. Behind him, the murder board.

"Thank you, girls and boys," he said, raising his hands in the air. The chatter quickly dropped away. "The reason you're all here is because we're going to make an arrest with respect to Valerie Usher's murder. We'll be taking down Duncan Usher himself." The officers were hanging on Copeland's every word.

"We've been waiting a long time for this, and now we've got the chance to make something stick and put him away for a long, long time. If we get this right, everyone present will be retired by the time Usher is up for parole. It'll be a major feather in our caps."

Your cap, thought Gray. The rest of us are just bystanders.

"We've got a golden opportunity to bring in many, if not all, of Usher's men. I have information that some of his lieutenants are in the Wellington pub, just around the corner. We'll be going in hot and heavy, which is why you're all here. He's not going to go down without a fight. Simultaneously there'll be raids undertaken at a number of properties owned by individuals in the gang. Besides Usher, there are two men in particular I want to sweep up."

Copeland turned to the board and pointed at two photographs. "Dean Telfer, ostensibly Usher's driver but also his minder and confidante, and Frank McGavin, a rising star in the Usher ranks. These, my friends, are the snakes. If we cut the heads off these people tonight, then the troops will be compliant. Any questions?"

Gray cleared his throat to speak. "What are the charges against Telfer and McGavin, sir?"

"Anything and everything, Constable Gray. We have no evidence they were involved in the attacks on Valerie Usher or Craig Mundby, but I do expect something to turn up from the parallel raids. Any other questions?"

Before Gray could continue, Carslake touched his arm and whispered, "Sol, leave it."

Nobody spoke. "Right, you'll be split into teams, each of which will have a specific task. We move in forty-five minutes. Good luck everyone."

The meeting broke up and suddenly they were all talking; considering the implications of Copeland's orders.

"Are you trying to get yourself into trouble?" asked Carslake.

"I don't believe he's considered the potential fallout, Jeff. If Usher doesn't want to come quietly, this could kick off trouble."

"He's the boss, remember?"

"How could I forget?"

"Make sure you don't. We're with Copeland. He wants his moment in the sun, and we're giving it to him."

"Yes, sir."

THE WELLINGTON PUB was down on a narrow, quiet backstreet, less than half a mile from the station. The silence was broken by the arrival of a line of police cars and vans, their blues off.

Uniform piled out the moment the vehicles drew to a halt, filling the road in front of the pub. Copeland had decided to forego the use of any riot gear, he reckoned it would make them look weak. Without waiting to see who was following, Copeland strode inside. Gray was only a few paces behind.

It appeared as if the clientele had frozen in their tracks, like a Western movie when a stranger enters the saloon, and everyone turns to glare. Gray scanned the room. Usher was at the bar; standing between Dean Telfer and another of his men called Larry Lost. There were about fifteen people inside, and at least twice as many cops. McGavin was nowhere to be found.

Copeland stood in the middle of the room, hands on hips, smile on his face. "Having fun are we, gentlemen?"

The temperature in the room plummeted. Although the cops outnumbered the pub's regulars, Gray picked out the shifting of nervous feet from his colleagues.

"What can I get you, Inspector?" said Usher, pushing his way through to stand a few feet away from Copeland; Telfer at his back. "There's a decent guest beer all the way down from Manchester."

"I'm not here to crack jokes."

"Shame, I've always found you rather amusing.

"Where's Frank?" asked Carslake making an obvious effort to look around the bar.

"He left earlier," piped up Larry.

"Shut up!"

Larry's face dropped.

Usher turned back to Copeland. "So, if this isn't a social visit, what is it?"

"I'm here to arrest you, Mr Usher."

"On what charge?"

"For the murder of your wife."

Usher blinked, taken aback.

"You see all these officers behind me?" Copeland hiked a thumb over his shoulder. "They're here in case of trouble. I've more outside."

"I hope you've brought the riot gear."

"Yes, and a water cannon." Copeland took a pace forward. "I'm really hoping you'll be a problem, because then I can add resisting arrest to your charge sheet."

"I've done nothing wrong."

"Right now, gentlemen, some of your houses are being raided. I'm sure we'll find something of use. So, are you lot coming quietly or loudly?"

Usher raised his hand as his men began to protest. "Everybody, this is a simple case of harassment. Go quietly."

"Pity," said Copeland, looking genuinely disappointed. He turned to Gray. "Cuff him."

Thirty One

Now Gray was pushing his peas around the plate, struggling to work up an appetite. Rain dappled the windows, and low clouds hung over the horizon. The intercom buzzed. He dropped his fork and went to see who was calling. On the black and white monitor, Fowler was staring up at him, his features magnified and distorted by the fisheye lens. Nose large, chin tiny. Gray let him in, opened the front door, and awaited his arrival.

Fowler fell through, landing hard on the floor. He curled himself up and began giggling. Gray bent over him and managed to help him stand, reeling at the stench of alcohol and sweat coming off him. Fowler wasn't just drunk, he was hammered. And he was wet. His suit was soaked through, his hair plastered across his scalp. His tie was askew, his shirt open halfway down his chest, a couple of buttons missing.

"I've left her," he slurred. "Bitch." As if Gray needed an explanation.

"Come and sit down." Gray led him to the sofa. His motion was an erratic weave, more sideways than forwards.

Gray went back and closed the front door. "Why?"

"Why what?"

"Why did you leave her?"

"Had enough." Fowler slumped sideways onto the sofa. "Didn't know where else to go, mate. Got any booze?"

"I'll find you something."

Gray went into his kitchen and made a coffee. He stuck a couple of sugars in before taking it out to Fowler who sat up and eyed it suspiciously. "What's that?"

"Coffee. It's got brandy in it," Gray lied.

"Good man." Fowler took the drink. "I thought for a minute you were trying to sober me up." He hiccupped.

"Never." Gray waited while Fowler sniffed the coffee and took a cautious slurp. Gray hoped the sugary taste would mask the fact there was no alcohol present. Fowler didn't complain. "What's going on, Mike?"

"I've left Yvonne, the bitch," repeated Fowler. He lay back on the sofa, legs spread, arms along the back, his eyes towards the ceiling. "She started shouting at me last night after I got home, so I walked out. Went to the pub until they threw me out. Went to a club until that shut."

"Where did you sleep?"

"On a bench. Then I headed to the Flag as soon as it opened." The English Flag was a notoriously down-at-heel pub near the station in the Old Town of Margate. "You said I could come round if anything happened. Well, I've run out of money and lost my wallet, wanted to borrow some cash. Share a drink with my old mate first." He raised his mug.

"I've got a spare bed, you can crash here."

"Cheers."

"Did you pack a bag before you left?"

Fowler tried to focus on Gray. "Nope."

"I've got some clothes you can borrow."

"Cheers, you're a mate," said Fowler again.

"I'll make the bed."

Gray went to put some sheets on the bed. When he returned the sofa was empty. Fowler was in the kitchen going through Gray's cupboards. "Looking for the brandy," he said.

"You had the last of it."

"Crap." Fowler rubbed a hand across his face. He slumped down onto the floor, leaning back against a cupboard for support. "I've fucked up, Sol."

Gray sat down beside him. The floor was cold. "I'm sure when you wake tomorrow everything'll be all right."

Fowler burst into tears, heavy sobs wracking his chest. Gray didn't know what to do. He put a hand on his shoulder and squeezed, whatever good that would achieve.

"It's all too much. Destroying my marriage for Yvonne, moving in with her, then that collapsing. It's been for nothing. God, what have I done?"

Gray couldn't answer. He sat beside his friend until Fowler wiped his face with a sleeve, pushed himself up, and staggered to the front door. "I shouldn't have come round."

"Where else do you have to go, Mike?"

He thought for a long moment. "Nowhere."

Gray led him to the spare bedroom. "I'll get you something to sleep in."

"Okay." Fowler collapsed onto the bed.

Gray fetched an old t-shirt for him, but when he came back Fowler was comatose on top of the bed, fully clothed. Gray folded the duvet over him before going out onto the balcony and standing under the overhang, out of the worst of the rain.

He found Hamson's number on his mobile then dragged the French window closed.

The call went through to voicemail. He tried again, same result. He sent a text. "Mike is with me."

Hamson rang him straight back. "How is he?"

"Snoring on my spare bed."

"Thank God for that. Drunk?"

"Maybe a little."

"What a surprise." Hamson sighed heavily. Gray wasn't sure whether it was in frustration or sadness. "I thought you were trying to call me after your suspension, to justify yourself."

"In the past I would have, Von, but we're hardly on strong footing these days."

"I guess not. What are you going to do?"

"Best you don't know."

"Thanks, by the way."

"What for?"

"Looking after him."

"He's a friend, Von, it goes without saying. Like I would for you, too."

There was a long pause down the line. "I've got to go, Sol."

Thirty Two

Then
Copeland rocked back in his chair, hands in his trouser pockets, regarding his quarry on the other side of the table. A folder, closed for now, lay on the surface within Copeland's reach. Gray took the traditional stance, all four chair legs on the floor as did Carslake beside him. Before Gray was a pad of paper and a pen.

The room was too warm. The central heating system had been turned on in late September at autumn's apparent onset. But the decision had been too hasty. The unseasonable snap had caught them out. The radiator itself was off, but the large pipes feeding it were filled with hot water which gurgled and knocked as it flowed. And five bodies in the room each contributed a few degrees.

Usher appeared cool and collected; a half smile on his lips, seemingly unaffected by the temperature. A bead of sweat rolled down Copeland's forehead. He raised a hand and wiped it away. To Gray this seemed to be a bigger deal for his inspector than the man with a murder allegation hanging over his head.

Rufus Dowling, Usher's lawyer, was more sensibly dressed in casual chinos and a white shirt, open at the neck, loafers and no socks. He appeared as if he'd just walked off a yacht, his shock of ginger hair fashioned into a seemingly windswept style, though Gray would bet the mound wouldn't shift in a breeze. Like Gray, Dowling was prepared to take notes. A pen lay next to his rimless glasses on the pad.

"Let's get this done," said Copeland. He leaned over, started the recorder. Copeland stated the date, time, and the names of the five people in the room. Dowling put on his glasses, perching them on the end of his nose, ready now.

"Here we are, Duncan," said Copeland.

"Please refer to my client as, Mr Usher or sir, Inspector Copeland," said Dowling.

"Of course. My apologies." Copeland didn't sound sorry in the slightest. "When we spoke on Saturday night, Mr Usher, you told me and my colleagues you were getting back together with Valerie."

Usher leaned forward "It's Mrs Usher to you. My wife's dead and you feel it's okay to be on first-name terms with her? Tosser."

Copeland's mouth flapped like a landed fish.

Carslake took over, saving his boss from further embarrassment. "We're asking, Mr Usher, because we subsequently heard your wife had no interest in resurrecting the marriage."

"Whoever told you that didn't know us very well."

"So Mrs Usher's mother, who lives nearby and regularly sees her daughter isn't aware of her own daughter's feelings?"

"What Eva sees and what she says are often two different things, Jeff." Usher had adopted a bored tone. Gray wouldn't be surprised if Usher started inspecting his fingernails soon.

Copeland stepped back in, his composure regained. "You're saying she's lying?"

"In her own mind, no. She doesn't like me and never has. Therefore, her perception is biased."

Copeland paused, seemingly thinking. Gray noted Usher's response. Dowling scratched away at his pad, too. Here was a difference between two witness accounts – something for the legal teams to pick at, should Usher ever go to court. Copeland let the seconds stretch until eventually he said, "Did you have sex with your wife yesterday?"

"What's the relevance of this highly personal question, Inspector?" asked Dowling, peering at Copeland over his glasses, pinching the skin above his nose into a frown. Outwardly, Usher seemed not to react, but Gray caught a brief tightening of his mouth.

"We have physical evidence that Mrs Usher had sexual intercourse shortly before her death. If it wasn't with you, Mr Usher, she clearly had someone else on the side."

Usher didn't answer.

"Did the pair of you have sex previously?" repeated Copeland.

"Of course, we had two children."

Dowling laughed.

"I meant," said Copeland, "since you separated."

"Yes."

"How often?"

Usher crossed his arms. "Whenever Val felt like it."

"And on the day you visited her last?"

"No, the children were there, it was the afternoon, it would have been inappropriate."

"Someone did. Any idea who?"

Dowling put a hand on Usher's forearm. "Inspector, I protest at your current line of questioning, it's improper."

Copeland, taking his time again, flipped open the folder revealing a small pile of glossy photos. He spread them out on the table between himself and Usher, images of Valerie's body – long shots of the bed and close ups on her neck, revealing the bruising in brutal clarity. Copeland closed the folder then nudged several of the prints closer to Usher.

"Take a good look, Duncan." Usher glanced down at one before turning away, directing his eyeline towards a wall.

"Strangled. A very personal process. It means getting up close. Why'd you kill her?"

"I didn't."

"I have evidence which says otherwise."

"What evidence?" said Dowling.

"We'll come to that momentarily." Copeland made no move to clear away the photos. "Craig Mundby. You said when we last spoke you thought he was a good kid."

"That's right, his heart's in the right place, and he's funny."

"You know he was found next to your wife?"

"There's no way Craig was involved, Inspector. He wouldn't hurt a fly. I've watched him play with my girls on many occasions. He's gentle with them."

"Craig's own mother has described him as not respecting others' boundaries. Very trusting of you to let him play with your girls."

"I never found him to be a problem."

Copeland opened the folder and withdrew another couple of photos from the folder. He swept Valerie's photos to one side. "This is the aftermath of Craig's apparent suicide attempt."

Copeland placed the first image down onto the table. It was a shot of the floor beside Valerie's bed.

"The large stain is his blood. He used a knife from Valerie's kitchen to cut himself." The next photo was of the weapon itself in-situ."

"What's this got to do with my client?" asked Dowling.

"I'm coming to that, Mr Dowling. When my colleagues entered the house, they found Craig bleeding out. Thankfully his life was saved. However, the post mortem produced a disparity. Mrs Usher had been dead for approximately an hour, and it appears Craig was with her for most if not all of this time. Why? Was it a case of him gradually filling with remorse before deciding the best way out was to cut himself?"

"Shouldn't you be asking Craig that, Inspector?"

"We have. Mr Usher, I think you knew your wife was having an affair, and that was a problem for you. Compared to your two girls she wasn't so important – they were what mattered. You said yourself when we spoke you'd maintained a cordial relationship just for them. If Mrs Usher divorced you, it would have been a racing certainty she'd get custody of the girls. I think she told you she was getting off with her new man and was moving a long way from you."

"That's not what happened."

"I know you doted on them, Mr Usher." Copeland put another photo on the table, this one of Elodie and Lotty, both smiling for the camera. It was an image from the mantelpiece in Mrs Usher's house. "Thank God they weren't murdered in their beds too, eh? You hatch a plan to kill her and frame somebody else, our poor Craig Mundby?"

"None of this is true. I wouldn't put Craig in the picture for murder, he's a decent person."

"Did he like you?"

"I'd hope so."

"Which is interesting also, because we have a statement that Craig was enticed into Mrs Usher's house. By you."

"Bullshit," said Usher.

Dowling placed a hand on Usher's forearm. He shook it off. "That's a lie. I wasn't even in the area."

"Can anyone corroborate that?" asked Copeland.

"You know they can't."

"This is conjecture, Inspector," said Dowling.

"Do you know Raptor Security?"

"Yes, they've done some work for me in the past."

"At your wife's house?"

"Yes."

"Which was another aspect that bothered me. The security around the property. There's lots of it. Way more than would ordinarily be needed in an area like the Chessboard. It's hardly Gotham City. Seems strange. What would Mrs Usher be so scared of, I wonder? Yet when we arrive, the security is disabled. The gate is wide open, the alarm off. All the defences rendered useless.

"When we spoke to Raptor they told us something very interesting. The specification was detailed by you, Mr Usher. You paid for everything."

"So? It's not unusual for working husbands with a stay-at-home wife."

"What about the access codes?"

"My wife changed them."

"Yes, though there's an override in case of emergencies. And you had that too. Meaning no matter what Mrs Usher altered the codes to, or how often she changed them, you could bypass them. You could walk right in whenever you wanted."

Usher didn't respond.

"How often have you been to your wife's house?" asked Copeland.

"Quite a few times."

"You know it well, then."

"Reasonably."

"We found your hair and fingerprints all over the house."

"My client has already disclosed he visited Mrs Usher's residence," said Dowling.

"Yet the bedroom was clean. We couldn't find evidence present. Nothing, Mr Usher. Not even your wife's hair or fingerprints. Every surface had been wiped and the floor vacuumed. Even the hoover had been emptied and the contents taken away. That wouldn't have been a quick process." Copeland turned to Carslake. "How long did we estimate it would take, Sergeant Carslake?"

"Fifteen to twenty minutes."

"Fifteen to twenty minutes," repeated Copeland. "For one person to be thorough. Which starts to explain the gap between Valerie's time of death and Craig's seeming suicide attempt."

"Why would Mr Usher bother to remove traces of himself from his wife's bedroom when he's already said he slept with her several times. Clearly the fact that the killer tried to remove any trace of themselves points to some other than Mr Usher."

"Your client has already stated that he didn't have sex with Mrs Usher that day. Somebody clearly did. We believe that to be your client. During the post mortem the pathologist found organic material under Valerie's fingernails. We analysed the material then compared it to our database. It came up with a highly probable match. Which was you, Mr Usher."

Copeland sat back and smiled.

"I need some time with my lawyer," said Usher.

"Take all you need." Copeland stood, pushing his chair back with a scrape.

Out in the corridor Copeland briskly rubbed his hands together, a grin on his face. "We've got him! I can feel it."

After the stuffy interview room, Gray wanted a change in scene. He found Fowler already outside in the car park, a cigarette half gone. He offered Gray the packet and a light. Gray hadn't smoked for a while, but he accepted. He inhaled a lungful of dirty air, hung onto it for a few long seconds, then blew it out.

"What a crazy day," said Fowler. "Usher's lot haves been kicking off constantly. How's it going with the man himself?"

"He's consulting with his lawyer."

"Must be good then."

"Copeland's pleased."

"Copeland's not often wrong, and if he's sure Usher's the perpetrator, that's enough for me." Fowler finished his cigarette, dropped the end on the floor and ground it out. "Still enjoying it after the big step up to CID?"

"Early days so far." Gray was glad of the change in subject.

"What about Wonder Boy?"

Fowler meant Carslake, who'd enjoyed a rapid rise through the ranks, far faster than either Gray or Fowler.

"He's fine."

The door from the station opened. "Speak of the devil," said Fowler, as Carslake stepped outside. "I'll see you later; don't forget the offer of that beer." Fowler retreated inside, Carslake holding the door open for him.

"Thought you'd given up," said Carslake.

Gray held up the cigarette. "I have." He took another drag, the ember glowing bright. "Are we going back in already?"

"They're still talking. I just wanted to say I think you've done a great job with this case."

"It's not over yet."

"We're on the last lap though, Sol."

"Can you feel that, too?"

Carslake laughed briefly. "Do you mind if I give you some advice?" Gray shrugged. "I know Copeland behaves like a superior prick, but if you keep your head down, get on with your work, and follow the DI's lead, it'll all be fine in the end."

"For who?" Gray stubbed out his cigarette.

"Everybody."

"Copeland, you mean."

Carslake shook his head then said, "Look, Copeland is going places. It won't be long, particularly once he gets Usher, and someone else will be in his chair. Just put up with him for now."

Thirty Three

Now When Gray checked on Fowler, he found the duvet thrown back and no Fowler. Gray went through the flat, from one room to another. When he reached the bathroom, the door was closed.

"Mike? Are you in there?" Gray knocked. No answer. He put his ear to the door. Nothing. "Mike!" Still nothing. Gray rattled the handle, the door was locked. He put a shoulder to the door and pushed. It didn't budge. He stepped back, raised his leg and stamped his foot against the wood, adjacent to the handle. Two good kicks, and the lock splintered. A third and the door burst open. Fowler was slumped in the bath, fully clothed. He'd removed his tie and dropped it beside the bath. Fowler's eyes were closed. The medicine cabinet above the sink stood open. Several pill bottles lay on the edge of the bath beside him. Gray couldn't move.

This must have been how it looked to Carslake when he'd found Gray. He'd clambered in the bath, arranged pill bottles along the edge the same as Fowler. He'd had a bottle of vodka to wash everything down with. But Gray hadn't been able to do it. Fowler had.

Gray jerked himself into action. He knelt down and pushed two fingers onto Fowler's neck. There was a pulse. A quick check of the bottles revealed one was paracetamol, the others were his cancer drugs. Only the paracetamol bottle was open though. He ran back into the living room, grabbed his phone and dialled 999. "Police emergency," said Gray and identified himself. "I need an ambulance right now." Gray gave his address. "I've got a pulse, but he's unresponsive."

"What's wrong with the patient?" asked the call handler, a man with a deep voice.

"He's unconscious after taking some pills, paracetamol."

"Make sure he stays upright, wait for the paramedics to arrive, and try to keep him conscious if you can."

Gray disconnected, opened the front door and returned to the bathroom. He grabbed hold of Fowler's lapel and pulled him into a sitting position. Gray checked his pulse again. Fowler groaned then threw up all over himself.

"Mike, I'm here." Gray slapped Fowler round the face, gagging with the stench of vomit which was powerful in the confined space. Fowler groaned, and his eyelids fluttered open. He tried to focus on Gray before his eyes rolled back into his head once more.

Gray waited for the paramedics to arrive. He kept glancing at his watch, the second hand ticking round painfully slowly. It felt like hours but was really only minutes. Fowler groaned several times, giving Gray hope, but he felt powerless, unsure what to do for the best. All he could do was follow the handler's advice.

Gray heard movement in the flat. He stood as two paramedics in green, one carrying a black medical bag, crowded the small room. "Can we get through please," said a woman, dark hair shot with white. Her sleeves were rolled up as if she meant business. She was pushing a stretcher.

"It's an overdose," said Gray as he shifted into the hallway. "Paracetamol."

"How many did he take?"

"About twenty."

"In one go?"

"I think so."

The woman turned and looked over her shoulder. "Can you wait in the living room?" The paramedics bent over and proceeded to look Fowler over as Gray withdrew, leaving Gray with the stretcher.

Gray rang Hamson while he waited.

"It's Mike," he said when she answered. "He's taken some pills."

"Oh my God."

"There's a paramedic crew working on him now."

"I'm coming over."

"There's no point, we'll have left for the hospital by the time you arrive."

"I'll see you there." Hamson disconnected.

The paramedic re-emerged into the room, making for the stretcher.

"How is he?" asked Gray.

"We're going to have to pump his stomach back at the hospital and administer an antidote to counteract the paracetamol," she said.

The stretcher with Fowler lying on it, half under a blanket, emerged into the living room. Fowler's eyes were closed, his face pale as ash. They'd stuck a drip into his arm, the bag hanging from a hook.

Gray turned to one of the paramedics. "Can I come in the ambulance with you?"

"Hurry up then."

Gray grabbed his mobile and pulled the door closed. He stepped into the lift, a tight squeeze beside the stretcher. The lift doors shut, and the box descended.

Thirty Four

T**hen**

"Is that thing off?" Usher pointed to the recorder.

Dowling bent over and checked. "Yes."

"I have to confess."

"When we discussed the accusation earlier you were adamant about your innocence!"

"And I still am. Whatever Copeland claims was found under Val's nails isn't from me."

"That's good, then we'll be able to cast doubt in the jury's minds."

"I've been set up. When Val was being murdered I was elsewhere. I just can't prove it."

"I know, you were in your flat."

"No, I was in a garage."

"So what?"

"I was murdering a man."

Dowling stood up, ran his fingers through his hair. "Fucking hell, Duncan!"

"There were two witnesses to that particular act. I've a choice now. Either I go down for Val's death or I own up to where I actually was and take everybody with me. I can't let that happen."

Dowling flopped into his seat again. "What do you want me to do?"

"Nothing. I've made my decision already. You're going to call Copeland back in. We're not going to offer a defence against his accusation."

"Are you going to confess?"

"No, I'm just shutting down. The cops can come to whatever conclusions they like, as long as it doesn't come out what I was actually up to. Okay?" Dowling didn't answer, staring sullenly at him. "You have to do this, Rufus. If not I'll have you replaced by another lawyer who will. If I feel I can't trust you..." Usher let the threat hang in the air.

Eventually Dowling said, "I'll get Copeland."

Usher smiled to himself. He'd been outmanoeuvred. He just didn't know who by.

Thirty Five

N^{ow} The ambulance journey was fast and steady. Gray rocked around in the back, seated at Fowler's feet, while the female paramedic perched beside him. He heard the sirens go on just the once before they took what felt to be the roundabout on the edge of Broadstairs. Right now a smooth, efficient ride was of the essence. The emergency services only thrashed it on the way to a scene.

The moment they drew up, the paramedic was past Gray and opening the doors. She and her colleague wheeled Fowler out, the legs of the stretcher extending to hit the ground outside. Then they were gone, moving fast, Gray trailing in their wake.

Inside, a nurse pointed Gray to a waiting area. It took half an hour before a doctor emerged. His white medical coat was open, revealing jeans and a casual shirt, chest hair spilling out above the top button. The man, who introduced himself as Dr Zaika, spoke with an Eastern European inflection.

"How's Mike?" asked Gray.

Zaika ran his hand through his long, centre parted hair. "We've stabilised him for now."

Gray blew out a lungful of air. "That's a relief."

"Mr Fowler is by no means in the clear though. Paracetamol is one of the least effective drugs a person can use to attempt suicide. It rarely kills, and a high dose can damage the liver."

"And?"

"We don't know yet, we're going to test his liver function shortly. The main task initially was to pump Mr Fowler's system clear, which we've done."

"Can I see him?"

"Mr Fowler doesn't want visitors right now. Can I suggest you return tomorrow?"

Gray called for a taxi, as his car was still at his flat. While he waited outside, he rang Hamson – she'd been a no show – but it immediately dropped into voicemail. The taxi arrived within a few minutes.

When Gray reached his flat he found Hamson sitting on the floor outside his door.

"You've got some nosey neighbours," she said. "I've had to show my badge twice while I was waiting for you."

"Why didn't you come to the hospital?"

"I couldn't."

Gray slid his key into the lock and opened up. "Come in."

"I need a cigarette," she waved a packet at him. "Can I smoke on your balcony?"

"I thought you'd given up?"

Hamson extracted a stick and jabbed it between her lips. "Fuck off, Sol." She flicked the lighter and sucked hard, burning the first centimetre of the stick. She was all stiff angles and tension, like an Anglepoise lamp. She plumed white smoke into the air. "What a fucking idiot," she shook her head and took a mug from Gray.

"Maybe it was a cry for help?"

"Why take pills? Just talk!" Hamson ground out the half-smoked cigarette on the balcony floor. "It wasn't exactly the strongest basis for a relationship, moving in after he'd left his wife of two decades."

"I can't imagine living with Mike was easy."

"That's an understatement. Then again, neither am I. I've been on my own for so long."

"Makes two of us."

"But mine was by choice." Hamson realised what she'd said, a mortified expression crossed her face. "Sorry, I shouldn't have said that."

"I don't blame you."

"Like you didn't the last time we had coffee together? When I accused you of going after my job."

"I remember it well."

"Everything has been so tough, what with Mike, you, and Carslake."

"I'm sorry."

"Where did he do it?"

"The bathroom."

"Can I see?" Without waiting for his answer Hamson walked past Gray. Hamson bent down and picked up Fowler's discarded tie. "Is this yours?"

"It's Mike's."

"Good." Hamson took hold of the tie in both hands about the centre and yanked at it hard until there was a ripping sound and the fabric was in two pieces. She dropped them to the floor then leaned into the bath, picked up one of the bottles Fowler had discarded and read the label. Frowning she turned to Gray said, "What are these for?"

"Pain relief."

"They're not your basic paracetamol, Sol."

"Now's not the time, Von."

"You might as well tell me. I can Google the brand and find out anyway." Hamson pulled her phone out and began to tap away.

"I've got cancer."

Hamson stared at Gray wide-eyed. "Why didn't you say?"

"Would you have listened?"

"Jesus, you need to ask me that, Sol?" Gray didn't answer. "Are you going to be all right?"

"Probably."

Hamson stared at him for a long moment. "Can I trust you?"

"Yes, of course."

Hamson sat on the edge of the bath. "It's Carslake. He was talking to me earlier in the week. About you."

"It's happened more than once, Von. What's the big issue?"

Hamson shook her head, clearing cobwebs. "He was saying you had to go, that you only caused trouble, that I had to choose between you and my job." Carslake was playing him off against Hamson then. "I told him I'd think about it. You're a pain in the arse, Sol, and you always will be, but this isn't right. It's subterfuge and politics. Stabbing someone in the back. It's right up Carslake's street."

"Funny that, because Carslake said exactly the same to me," Gray said. "If you go, I get a promotion."

"And?"

"I said I'd think about it." Gray smiled, then he began to laugh. Hamson joined in.

"Oh my God," said Hamson after half a minute. "I needed that. It feels like an age since I last enjoyed myself."

"I don't believe Carslake anyway," said Gray. "I'm just a pawn. You've become a problem somehow and he wants rid of you, via me."

"What are you going to do when he comes asking? Because he's bound to."

"Tell him no."

"I need another cigarette."

Back on the balcony, while Hamson was sparking up, Gray said, "I've got a theory. Us not getting on plays into Carslake's hands. It's a divide-and-rule tactic. We have to keep up the play-act, which means you carry on pretending to be pissed off with me."

"That won't be too hard."

"I also think Carslake's throwing me under a bus with the IPCC. And Smits came clean, he told me the investigation doesn't centre on me, but Carslake."

"This is crazy." Hamson held her head in her hands. "Why?"

"Wish I knew. I need you to keep me up to date with what's happening at the station."

Hamson sat upright, nodded. "Of course."

"Are you going to see Mike?"

"I think I will."

Thirty Six

Then
  When Gray reached the interrogation room, he was aware his clothes reeked of cigarettes. Copeland glanced at him; his nose wrinkled. The five of them returned to the same seats. The room remained sweltering. Dowling appeared to be suffering the heat too, his face flushed. Copeland re-started the recording.

"Let's summarise, Mr Usher. We have proof of your presence at the crime scene."

"That doesn't make my client a murderer, Inspector," interrupted Dowling.

"Rufus," said Usher, "let the man speak."

"You had free access to the house, no witnesses to your whereabouts at the time of your wife's murder, and your DNA under her fingernails. And there's the witness statement from Craig Mundby that he was invited by you into Mrs Usher's house, placing you firmly at the scene."

Dowling had one arm of his glasses in his mouth, chewing on them.

"As I'm sure Rufus is aware, when we take a case to the CPS for review, they look at the strength of the evidence. In your case we tick all the boxes, several times. Means, motive, and opportunity. Duncan Usher, I'm arresting you for the murder of Valerie Usher, for the attempted murder of Craig Mundby, and for attempting to pervert the course of justice. Anything you say can and will be used in evidence against you in a court of law. Do you understand these charges?"

"Loud and clear, Inspector."

"Take him away, Sol."

LATER THAT EVENING, when Usher and his men had been processed, Copeland threw an impromptu celebration in the Britannia pub next door to the station. It was crammed with officers of the law. At the centre of it all was Copeland, basking in the praise and buying the beer.

Gray accepted a pint, simply because Copeland was paying, but stayed distant from the melee of self-congratulation and sycophantic adulation. Carslake found Gray in a corner at a table by himself facing the wall.

Carslake sat down. "You look like someone's pissed in your glass."

"You might be right. I don't have the best of tastes in my mouth, Jeff."

"As I said to you earlier, Sol, ride the Copeland wave. He'll be gone soon. We're just a stepping stone."

"The sooner the better." Gray pushed his half-drunk pint away. "Has McGavin turned up?"

"His lawyer says he's gone away on holiday. A last-minute booking."

"Convenient."

"Nothing deemed incriminating was found at his house, so he's in the clear."

"McGavin's not stupid. I'd have been amazed if he'd leave anything casually lying around."

"It's been known to happen."

Gray stood. "I'm going to head home. Kate and I need to talk. It's been a busy few days, and I've barely seen my family. I'd rather be with them than getting drunk with him."

"I don't blame you."

As Gray walked out, Copeland caught his eye and raised a glass. Gray didn't bother to respond.

Thirty Seven

N^{ow} Gray's phone bleeped. A text from Pennance asking Gray to call him back. He did so.

"I've found the Mundbys," said Pennance.

"Great, where?"

"They're in Rhosneigr, a small coastal village on Anglesey, it's an island just off the north Welsh coast."

"I know where Anglesey is."

"And they're living under a new name – Pitts, her maiden name. It's why I took so long to find them."

"When did they move?"

"Not long after Usher was sentenced."

Gray checked the location via the map app on his phone. "They've moved to the middle of nowhere."

"That's what I thought. I'll send you the details. Molly would prefer to talk via Skype. Can you do that?"

"I reckon I can just about manage."

"I strongly suggest you don't screw this up, Sol. I had to use all my powers of persuasion to get Molly to this point."

"Thanks for the advice, Marcus, I usually go around attempting to make every mistake I can."

Gray and Pennance said their goodbyes and disconnected. His mobile beeped with a text outlining Molly's details. Gray

saw the time Molly suggested, which was before his shift started in the morning.

GRAY ROSE WITH THE alarm, went into the bathroom,
and splashed some water over his face in an effort to wake himself up properly. He started up his laptop.

He'd sent Molly a request to share contact details through
Skype prior to heading to bed. He opened up the software.
Molly had responded. Gray checked his watch. Only a couple
of minutes to go.

At 6 a.m. Gray dialled. It rang but wasn't picked up. He
hoped she hadn't changed her mind. He tried again at five past.
Nothing. The moments ticked by. Gray, starting to worry, sent
her a quick instant message saying he was online and waiting.
At sixteen minutes past, Skype woke up. A video call was coming in.

Gray hadn't seen Molly since Usher's court case. She'd aged
of course; her hair had turned entirely grey. She was tanned.
Deep lines cut into her face. They appeared to be caused by
worry rather than laughter if the downturn of Molly's lips were
anything to go by. Molly's mouth was moving, but Gray
couldn't hear her. He switched on the speaker.

"... can't see you," said Molly. "Start your camera up."

"Okay, just a second."

Gray found the icon and clicked.

"That's more like it. Sorry I'm late, I was making sure Craig
was still asleep." Molly's tone wasn't particularly apologetic.

"Thanks for agreeing to speak with me."

"Your friend strongly suggested I should."

Gray wondered what lever Pennance had pulled; he didn't need to know.

"How's Craig?"

"He's fine. That's why I wanted to speak early so he doesn't overhear and isn't reminded of the past. We've worked hard to forget. And there you are."

"You're aware Duncan Usher has been released?"

A flicker crossed Molly's face. Gray thought it was anxiety. "Your colleague told me. It hasn't made the news here. I never thought I'd see the day. Life without parole, they said." Molly uttered a sharp laugh, devoid of humour.

"What about James?"

"He's probably in bed. He didn't want to leave Thanet so I left him."

"I'm sorry to hear that."

"Don't be." Molly waved Gray's concern away. "It was hard at the time, but I guess all those people's predictions about us not lasting were true after all."

"Why Anglesey?"

"We fancied a change." The sarcasm was obvious.

"Buying a new shirt is a change, moving to the other side of the world is significant." Gray tried to dig. "You moved to get as far away from him as possible."

"Not quite, Sergeant. We wanted to get as far away from everything as possible."

"I don't blame you."

"Got yourself involved in a life-threatening situation with a major criminal recently have you?"

"Not for a while."

"Then you won't know what it's like." Molly turned her face away from the camera and squeezed her eyes shut. "It took Craig months to recover physically, but up here." She faced forward again and tapped her temple. "He's never been like he used to be. He still has the scars on his wrist as a reminder of that day. Even going to the other side of the world, as you said, can't get Craig away from what's in his head and on his body. I always liked the idea of living in the middle of nowhere, and Craig nearly dying made me realise we should get on with it while we could."

"How's it been?"

"Tough at first, then things improved as we settled, hard again when I left James but the last few years have been pretty good. I've met someone else who gets on great with Craig, and I've got a decent job at a local school. I just hope all of this with Usher resurfacing doesn't knock my life off track again. I don't think I can go through that kind of upheaval once more."

"There's an investigation underway over here, into Usher's arrest and conviction. It possibly wasn't him who attacked Craig."

"So who was it?"

"That's why I wanted to speak with you. I'm trying to find out."

"If I help, will we get left alone?"

"Maybe, though I couldn't say for sure."

"I've had a man called Smits trying to get hold of me."

"He's a senior investigator examining the case."

"So it's being taken seriously then?"

"Yes, very."

A flicker of something crossed Molly's face.

"What is it, Molly?"

She shook her head. "I don't want any trouble for Craig. He's still fragile."

"I may be able to help."

"How?"

"I'll talk to Smits for you. But you need to be straight with me."

"Craig admitted he might have got something wrong."

"Wrong about what?"

Molly paused, Gray held his tongue until she said, "The man who called him inside, it wasn't Duncan Usher."

"Who then?"

"He doesn't know. It was dark. The lights were off." Gray wanted to swear. "But he's certain it wasn't Usher."

"Why didn't he say so at the time?"

"He couldn't. When Craig was hanging around on the street he saw someone go into Valerie's house on more than one occasion. Including the night she was murdered."

"Who?"

"That's why he couldn't say. He was threatened with prison if he spoke up."

"Who, Molly?"

"Sergeant Carslake."

After Molly had gone, Gray sat staring out to sea for some time, seeing nothing, realising everything.

He picked up his mobile and dialled Usher. "I know who set you up."

Thirty Eight

Then
   The trial had been underway for ten long weeks, but finally, it was judgement day. Literally. From the outset, Usher pleaded not guilty to the accusation of murder, attempted murder, and perverting the course of justice. Two days ago, the case had been summed up by both prosecution and defence. Before sending the jury away to a hotel room for deliberation, Judge Hewish stated she would accept a majority verdict.

The media scrutiny had proven intense, the crime generating huge public interest. Newspaper sales climbed on the back of the story of a crime boss turned wife killer. Usher was vilified in the papers, a heartless murderer who'd also attempted to slaughter and frame an innocent young man who'd been left physically and emotionally scarred for life as a result. In their eyes, Usher was guilty before he'd even been tried. Consequentially, finding an unbiased jury was difficult. And front and centre throughout stood Detective Inspector Copeland. He was the hero, the tough guy who'd brought a swift resolution to such a brutal case with his no-nonsense style.

When it was Gray's turn on the stand, he'd given evidence over a full day, cross examined by both sides. It was his debut and it proved stressful. The case against Usher had been solidly built by Copeland and supported by the Crime Prosecution Service.

Now, Gray was seated towards the rear of the packed-out public gallery. Copeland and Carslake had front-row seats, either side of Eva Franklin. Valerie's children were not in court to hear judgement – as had been the case throughout the trial. Defence and prosecution were in their places; Usher too, Dowling, beside him.

The jury filed in, followed a few moments later by Judge Hewish garbed in her formal gowns and wig. When Hewish was in her high-backed seat, she turned and said, "Foreman of the jury, have you come to a decision?"

The foreman, a shaven headed, tattooed man rose. "We have, your honour."

"And is a majority in favour?"

"We are, your honour."

"Against the charge of attempted murder, how do you find the accused?"

The room was deathly quiet. Eva gripped Copeland's arm.

"Guilty."

"And against the charge of murder, how do you find the accused?"

"Guilty."

There were loud gasps in the court. Eva Franklin sagged; seemingly relieved justice was done for her daughter. Usher didn't react.

"The court will reconvene in five days' time," said Hewish, "when a sentence will be handed down." The judge rose and made her way out. Usher was quietly led away.

The court burst into discussion. Eva hugged Copeland, then Carslake before the trio filed out. Doubtless there would be another media scrum on the court's front steps for Copeland. Gray couldn't face it.

LATER IN THE EVENING, Gray was in his London first-floor hotel room, fixing his tie before a mirror in the harshly lit bathroom. He would rather be doing anything other than going for a celebratory dinner with Copeland, even if the restaurant was Michelin-starred and someone else was paying. But as Carslake kept telling him, the boss was the boss.

Earlier, Gray had caught Copeland's interview on the television immediately after Usher had been found guilty, Eva Franklin by his side.

At the last possible moment, Gray headed downstairs, out through the lobby and onto the pavement. He was staying just along from Marble Arch, the hum of traffic constant and the tang of diesel fumes in the spring air. Gray headed in the direction of the monument. The restaurant, Icelandic in theme and fish the main ingredient, lay beyond the arch on a back street, away from the hubbub of vehicles. It took Gray a couple of minutes to walk there. He didn't rush.

The maître d' took Gray's coat before showing him to their table which was located towards the rear and beside the kitchen; glass-fronted so the diners could observe the chefs at work.

"I was beginning to believe you'd got lost." Copeland, already seated, was well dressed in a three-piece suit. Gray was perfectly on time.

"Wouldn't miss it for the world, sir," lied Gray.

"Jeff's just in the bathroom, powdering his nose. Ah, here he is now." Carslake sat down, said hello to Gray. "I took the liberty of ordering us a bottle of wine. I assume you're both okay with Sancerre." Copeland spoke in a way which indicated Carslake and Gray would be all right with it regardless.

"Yes, sir," said Carslake, adjusting his tie.

"First name terms only tonight, Jeff, please. This is a celebration! Me and my boys together, we cracked the case. So this is to us." Copeland raised his moisture dappled glass. They clinked.

The chilled wine was rich and deep. Gray didn't want to like the wine because Copeland had ordered it, but it was excellent. He was handed a menu and took a few minutes to make a selection. He held back from ordering the most expensive item just for the hell of it when the waiter returned. However, even the cheaper dishes were a significantly higher price than anything he'd find in a Thanet restaurant.

"Good choices," said Copeland to Gray after he'd selected.

Gray was surprised that during the meal Copeland kept the conversation away from the Usher case and himself. He was good company, with plenty of stories and anecdotes. Gray found himself warming to the man. The food was superb, and the trio went through several bottles. They finished with dessert and an accompanying sweet wine before Copeland ordered them all espressos and a decent cognac.

"How was that?" asked Copeland.

"I really enjoyed it, sir. Sorry, Terry. Thanks."

"You're welcome." The waiter delivered the coffee and digestive. Gray sipped the espresso, getting a jolt as the caffeine kicked in, adding to the warm feeling in his stomach. Copeland nipped at the brandy.

"Between us, I understand the judge is going to hand down the maximum sentence to Usher: life without parole. And they're going to seize his assets. Usher will be a broken man. It's all worked out rather well."

"So it seems," said Carslake.

"Don't think this is the last time we'll be sitting together and celebrating, gentlemen. I predict we'll crack plenty more cases together, us three. We're a team. Frankly, I wasn't sure about you at first, Sol, but you proved me wrong. You knuckled down, did as I asked, when I asked it. That's what I need in my people."

Copeland planted a hand on Gray's shoulder. "Jeff told me to stick with you, and he was right." Copeland raised his glass to Carslake who responded in kind. "Would your family consider a relocation, Sol?"

That caught Gray by surprise. "I hadn't thought about it to be honest. My wife is a local. She has lots of friends in the area, particularly through church."

"She's the God-fearing kind?" Copeland spoke as if religion were witchcraft.

"Kate believes, yes."

Copeland pulled a face, which rankled with Gray. Although he no longer believed, others had the right to do so. "Anyway, plenty of places to bend the knee to hoodoo around the country."

"What are you suggesting, Terry?"

"After this I'm expecting a promotion. Not immediately, but it'll come. It can't be in Thanet, the place is too small for me. I'd like to take you two with me as my wing men because you get my methods. It'll mean uprooting your families, but that's to be expected in the police. It's no different in the private sector. Go where the jobs are, right?"

Neither Carslake or Gray responded. Gray knew Carslake was ambitious, but family was extremely important to him as well. Gray felt lightheaded after all the booze. And the resurfacing of Copeland's narcissism in the last quarter of an hour meant the positivity he'd begun to feel towards him evaporated.

Gray stood up. "Thank you for dinner, sir, but I'm tired and I'm off to bed."

Copeland blinked in surprise. "Is this you turning me down, DC Gray?"

"I'm afraid I think I'm going to, sir."

"That's a pity. I hope you don't regret your decision."

"Somehow I doubt it, sir."

Gray left the restaurant and walked back to the hotel.

Thirty Nine

N^ow Sylvia, Carslake's PA and 1950s throwback, looked up in surprise when Gray barged into the office.

"Sergeant!" she shouted, as Gray carried on into Carslake's office.

"Where is he?"

Sylvia stepped back, a hand bright with several colours of fingernail polish, across her mouth.

"He's not here."

"I can see that!"

"He's on a day off."

"At home?"

"No, taken his grandchildren to Dreamland, I think. Do you want me to call him for you?"

"Don't bother, I'll find him."

"You're suspended." It was Smits, standing in the doorway. He'd been in the cupboard-cum-office when Gray had marched past. "What are you doing here, Sergeant?" Momentarily, Smits attempted to block Gray's path, but when he saw the look on Gray's face he stepped aside.

Gray, bounding down the stairs, made a call on his mobile to Usher and told him where Carslake was, ignoring Smit's echoing shout after him. He slammed open the fire door at the rear of the station, leapt into his car and screeched out of the car park. He raced along the esplanade, weaving in and out of the traffic. At the clock tower roundabout, he went straight over without pause, causing several cars to slam on their brakes. He ignored the blare of horns.

The bright lights of the amusement arcades flashed by. A few hundred yards along was the entrance to Dreamland. Arlington House, a block of residential flats, loomed like a dirty iceberg overhead, casting a long shadow. Gray bumped the car up onto the pavement. He jumped out of the car and dashed to Dreamland's entrance, which was located down an alley. At the turnstile Gray held out his warrant card and pushed his way through.

Inside, he paused. The park wasn't very busy. Some families milled around, wandering between the rides – a mix of the past and the present. Dodgems, roundabouts, slides. The scenic railway, the loops and curves of the oldest rollercoaster in the country, was towards the rear. A Ferris wheel towered over everything. Gray jogged through the park, his head twisting from side to side, desperate to find him.

His mobile rang. It was Carslake.

"I know," said Gray.

"You don't."

"Where are you?"

"At the foot of the scenic railway." Carslake clicked off.

Gray found him off to one side of the railway where it was quieter and nobody passed by. Carslake was over the protective fence, standing near the tracks. Gray followed.

"Don't come any nearer, Sol," said Carslake when Gray was within six feet. Just then the carriages rattled by on the railway, hitting the bottom of a steep downward curve. The screams of the passengers apparently enjoying the fear were deafening for a few seconds.

"Where are your grandkids?" asked Gray.

"Juliette has them. We're back where it all started. Where's the time gone?"

"We were friends."

"We are friends. Sometimes events just overtake us. Ah, hello Duncan." Carslake smiled. "We're all here now." Usher stood next to Gray.

"Did you kill my wife?" asked Usher.

Carslake shrugged.

"She was his informant," said Gray. "Right, Jeff? There could be nobody better placed than the wife of the boss."

"How did you know?"

"Craig Mundby saw you going into Valerie's house. Repeatedly."

"Who?" Carslake thought for a moment. "Oh, the slow lad. I was lucky it was Craig and not Usher who saw me. I was stupid to screw somebody else's wife in their own house. How did you find out, Sol?"

Usher took a step forward, a thunderous look on his face. Gray put out a hand and stopped him. "Not yet."

"Sol's right," said Carslake. "There's more to discuss." Another set of carriages hammered by, forcing a pause. When it was gone Carslake continued, "Copeland was putting us all under pressure to get a result with Usher. And when Val fell into my lap, I took the opportunity. She was an amazing woman."

"You were sleeping with her?"

"I was, Sol."

Usher growled.

"What happened that day?"

"She wanted me to leave my wife and move in with her. It would have cost me everything. Job, family, reputation. I couldn't."

"She wouldn't take no for an answer," said Usher.

"Correct, Duncan. And I did say no. She'd got her mother to babysit girls, so we had the place to ourselves. I ignored the risk that Duncan could have turned up at any time, too taken with Valerie. God, my head was a whirl of emotions. She told me she wanted out from Duncan."

"And you were the ticket."

"So it seemed. I didn't plan to kill her. I'd gone round to tell her it was over. She persuaded me into bed, for old times' sake. I couldn't resist. There was something about her, something that made you want her."

"It's called weakness, Jeff," said Gray.

"Maybe. I still miss her, you know."

"And my children do too," said Usher, clenching his fists.

"I'm sorry for that, I really am. Afterwards, when we were in bed she told me to leave my wife. I told her I couldn't. Then came the tears, the threats. And then she was lying on her back, her eyes open, staring at the ceiling, my hands around her throat."

Usher took a step forward. Gray pushed him backwards. He felt the anger boiling off Usher and wasn't sure how much longer he could keep him in check. But Carslake didn't appear to notice. "I panicked. Sleeping with an informant was bad enough, but murder? I couldn't go to jail."

"You set up Craig Mundby to take the fall."

"Craig," laughed Carslake, shaking his head. "He was always so keen to please." Carslake paused as more carriages rattled past. "It's been hard, Sol. Keeping everything quiet all these years."

"My heart bleeds. Who helped you? McGavin?"

"Actually no. It was Copeland. I called him in a panic. He came round and told me everything was all right, that actually it played into his hands. He told me he'd clean the room then leave. When I arrived at the scene an hour later, officially on duty..." Carslake shuddered. "I hadn't expected to find Craig bleeding out. I almost threw up. I wanted to go to Val, I couldn't though. I had to get on with it. Ever since then I've been drawn deeper into doing things I didn't want to." Carslake sighed. "It's the echoes of the dead, Sol. They're with me all the time."

"What about Tom? What did you do to Tom?" Gray demanded.

"I protected him; made sure he was safe and always would be."

"Tom's alive?"

"Yes."

"Where is he?"

"I don't know. I didn't want to know. I gave him to somebody else to deal with."

Now it was Gray's turn to show his rage. "You destroyed my family, Jeff. My wife died because of you."

"And mine," said Usher.

"Several people have died because of me. They're just two more in a long list. I can't go to prison, Sol."

The rumble of the carriages approaching was getting louder, so were the shouts of the people aboard.

"You won't be," said Usher and gave Carslake an almighty shove, just as the train rattled past. Carslake's scream was cut off as he went underneath the wheels. Gray fell to his knees.

"He had information about Tom!"

Usher walked away, leaving Gray in a heap.

Forty

T**hen**

It was visiting time and Duncan Usher's "guest" was late. This was when family and friends saw the imprisoned for a brief period, the chance once a month to meet loved ones. The bright spot before they went back to another twenty-plus hours a day in a cell with two other men. For Usher it was different. He had a cell to himself, because he was deemed high risk. So Usher didn't even have the company of his fellow prisoners. That was okay, he wasn't the sharing type.

Usher sat alone at the table watching every movement in the crowded, noisy room. He'd developed the habit of being observant when previously inside, when he'd been much younger and more naïve. He'd learned fast back then. It paid to be cautious. To check out every motion, every noise, before committing to an action. Because an error could end up with him in the infirmary. The sounds of people echoed around the expansive rectangle – couples talking, children wailing, partners crying. It was a well of misery. Light entered the space via high, barred windows and overhead lights. A woman with a baby in pink seated herself at the next table opposite a man who was mainly muscle and tattoos. The hard face melted as he held hands with his daughter.

Frank McGavin finally appeared, threading his way between the tables. His eyes shifted constantly. Although it had only been a short few months since he'd last seen McGavin, it appeared he'd grown. His bearing was subtly stronger, his presence greater. The other prisoners noticed McGavin as he passed by. Not who he was, but what he was. McGavin pulled out a chair opposite. It had been evident on the phone when they spoke, too. Usher possessed an illicit mobile to allow the pair to continue to conduct business.

The two eyed each other briefly before McGavin stuck out a hand for Usher to shake.

He's becoming rather like me, thought Usher. Restrained, intelligent, calculating. It came with being the boss.

"You've plenty of company in here," said McGavin.

"I keep my distance. You know how it is." The pair tried not to meet face-to-face, there were too many ears. But there were some subjects that didn't do to be discussed over the phone.

"Yes."

Usher came to it, the big question. "Have you been in touch with Elodie and Lotty?"

"Eva wasn't keen on me speaking to them, but I'm persistent." McGavin grinned. Usher didn't. He was bursting for the information. "Eva insisted she be present, as she's now their legal guardian."

"For God's sake, Frank. What did they say?"

"I'm sorry, Duncan."

Usher was suddenly alone. The noise of his surroundings disappeared. Frank, the cons and their visitors, gone. Usher was by himself.

Usher felt a touch on his arm, then he was back in the room. "Are you all right?"

Usher couldn't speak. "Don't give up," said McGavin.

"Where's the point now?"

"Appeal your conviction."

"On what grounds?"

"Who cares? When you prove your innocence you can look your daughters in the eye, and they'll know it wasn't you." A bell rang to indicate visiting time was over. "I'll keep the business running." McGavin stood. "We all appreciate what you've done for us." He offered his hand to Usher. "I'll get you out, Duncan. I promise. Just keep fighting."

Usher didn't believe him.

Forty One

Now Gray felt wiped out. The treatment had hit hard this time.

"How are you feeling?" asked Hamson. She sat beside him, the obligatory bunch of grapes in her lap, something about them helping his body accept the chemo better.

"Crap."

"I got you these." She showed Gray the fruit.

"Thanks."

Hamson put the grapes on top of the cupboard next to Gray's head. "It's been a busy couple of days."

"For you and me both. Smits and Wyatt have gone."

"Good. How's Mike?"

"I don't know. I haven't seen him since he got out of hospital. He's taken some time off. We're finished though, I'm sure of that." Hamson shifted in her seat. "What happened by the railway?"

"We've been over this, Von." Moments after Carslake died, Hamson, Smits and a wash of uniform had arrived at Dreamland. "I told you, he was confessing to everything, and then jumped in front of the train. My guess, he was overcome with guilt."

"Nobody else was with you?"

"It was just me and Carslake."

Hamson eyed Gray for a long moment, but he remained impassive. "I've been offered promotion to Chief Inspector."

"Congratulations, you deserve it." And Hamson did.

"Leaving an Inspector's position vacant."

"Ironic, given Carslake's offer to the both of us."

"I'm not Carslake."

"No, you're not."

"Well?"

"I don't know, Von. I'll need to think about it. So much has changed."

"When you're back, we'll talk about it, okay?" she patted his shoulder.

"Sure."

"Somebody else is here to see you."

"Two visitors in one day? I'm being spoilt."

Hamson opened the door. In came Duncan Usher.

Forty Two

N^{ow} Hamson had left the pair to it, saying she had work to do.

"I brought grapes, but I see you already have some," said Usher.

"Seems to be the in thing."

"How many bunches do you have?"

"Now? Two."

"Popular as ever, Gray."

"It's Sol."

"You could have stopped me." Usher meant from killing Carslake.

"I'm not sure I could have. Maybe he deserved it."

Usher took a grape, popped it into his mouth. "We're joined at the hip now, you and me."

"We probably are."

"I'm seeing them tomorrow, Elodie and Lotty. And my grandson."

"What's his name?"

"Lazenby."

"I'm pleased for you, Duncan."

"Thanks."

"When I told you I'd help you find Tom if you got Val's killers, I meant it. When you're out of here, I have a friend who's got information."

Forty Three

Now Usher turned the car engine off. He'd picked up Gray from the hospital and driven him to Dartford. Telfer had stayed in Thanet. Gray looked up through the windshield at the high rise which stretched above him. Usher got out, Gray followed suit.

The wind off the Thames buffeted Gray. He could hear the traffic flowing along the M25. A couple of teenagers on BMXs watched them. Usher led Gray into the flats. In an airy lobby they silently awaited the lift.

The man who'd occupied the cell next to Usher lived on the 18th floor. Usher knocked on the door. An old woman opened it wide. Usher stepped inside, trailed by Gray.

"Just give me a moment," said Usher, leaving Gray in the narrow hallway.

"Would you like a cup of tea?" asked the old lady. She was standing in the entrance to what Gray assumed was the kitchen, silhouetted. She held a teapot in her hand.

"I'm not sure whether we'll be staying long enough," said Gray.

"I'll put the kettle on anyway." She disappeared.

Usher returned to Gray and nodded towards the living room. "Come on, you've got your audience."

Jeremy Templeton had a window view of the river from his armchair, a throne of sorts, facing outwards. He appeared to be a similar age to the woman who Gray assumed to be his wife. Templeton was bald and wore glasses. He was wrapped up in a blanket. He didn't offer Gray a hand to shake. "Sit." Templeton nodded to a chair which had been pulled over from a nearby dining table. Gray frowned. There was a vague familiarity to the old man.

Mrs Templeton returned with a tray. The teapot was on it, as were three mugs and a plate of digestives. She poured and handed the first mug to Jeremy. He took it, his hands crooked like claws. Gray accepted his. Mrs Templeton left them alone.

"You want to know about your son," said Jeremy. He shook a cigarette out from a packet and stuck it between his lips.

"Yes."

Jeremy lit the cigarette and blew out a plume of smoke. "Usually I don't talk to coppers, but I'm doing a favour for Duncan here. He says he had a deal with you."

"Yes."

"And I have a deal with him." Templeton nodded at Usher who remained standing, quietly at Gray's shoulder.

Templeton sucked in and expelled another lungful of cigarette smoke. "I used to know Jeff Carslake, years back. He was somebody else I owed. I don't like debts. Usually they have to be repaid with interest. Carslake wanted somebody lifted. Your son."

Gray sat forward. "You were at the fair?"

"That's right. I was a bit more handsome back then." Templeton chuckled. Neither Gray or Usher joined in. Templeton was entirely unfazed by their lack of response. He tapped some ash from the cigarette over the side of the armchair, it floated downwards like snowflakes. Maybe there was an ashtray below, but Gray couldn't see it.

"Did you take Tom?" Gray tensed. He felt a hand fall on his shoulder. Usher squeezed. Templeton saw and smiled.

"I did."

"Where is he?" Gray clenched his hands into fists. He wanted to scream.

Templeton switched his attention to Usher. "This makes us square."

"It does," said Usher.

Templeton lit another cigarette before he said, "Find Lewis Strang. He's a cop, and he'll know where to find your boy."

If you enjoyed Beg For Mercy I'd greatly appreciate it if you would write a review. They really help authors like me grow and develop.

Thanks! It means a great deal to me.

And if you want to sign up to a periodic newsletter with information on launches, special offers etc. (no spam!) then you can do so HERE[1].

In return is a *free* book in the Konstantin series, ***Russian Roulette***, a unique and gritty crime thriller featuring an ex-KGB operative living undercover in Margate.

Now read the next Solomon Gray novel

Bury The Bodies

Other Novels by Keith Nixon

The Solomon Gray Series
Dig Two Graves
Burn The Evidence
Beg For Mercy
Bury The Bodies
The Konstantin Series
Russian Roulette
The Fix
I'm Dead Again
Dark Heart, Heavy Soul
The DI Granger Series
The Corpse Role
The Caradoc Series
The Eagle's Shadow
The Eagle's Blood

About the Author

Keith Nixon is a British born writer of crime and historical fiction novels. Originally, he trained as a chemist, but Keith is now in a senior sales role for a high-tech business. Keith currently lives with his family in the North West of England.

Readers can connect with Keith on various social media platforms:

Web: http://www.keithnixon.co.uk
Twitter: @knntom[1]
Facebook: Keithnixonauthor[2]
Blog: www.keithnixon.co.uk/blog[3]

---

1.   https://twitter.com/knntom

2.   https://www.facebook.com/keithnixonauthor/

3.   http://www.keithnixon.co.uk/blog

Don't miss out!

Visit the website below and you can sign up to receive emails whenever Keith Nixon publishes a new book. There's no charge and no obligation.

https://books2read.com/r/B-A-BGNH-VBXW

BOOKS 2 READ

Connecting independent readers to independent writers.

Did you love *Beg For Mercy*? Then you should read *Bury The Bodies* by Keith Nixon!

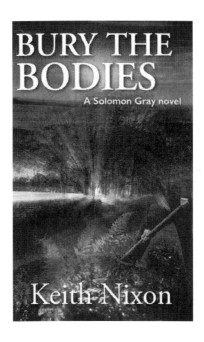

A missing son, a web of lies, a murder covered up. Detective Inspector Solomon Gray is getting closer to finding his son, missing now for over a decade. He's on the trail of a bent cop, Lewis Strang, who appears connected to the disappearance, all those years ago. But Strang is untouchable, a star of the Metropolitan police force. Once more, Gray must blur the line between right and wrong.When the body of a young black man turns up on a Margate back street it seems to be yet another drug related crime. Margate is currently the focus of a special operation, codenamed Pivot, to take down local suppliers. But Gray discovers there's more to the case than initially meets the eye.And Gray has his own problems to deal with. First there's the public investigation into the death of Gray's ex-boss, DCI Jeff Carslake and then Gray's estranged daughter, Hope, turns up on his doorstep – she's pregnant and left the child's father.**As Gray investigates he discovers the truth about Tom and who took him. A truth that is even more shocking than Gray ever expected...**Set in the once grand town of Margate in the south of England, the now broken and depressed seaside resort becomes its own character in this dark detective thriller, perfect for fans of Ian Rankin, Stuart MacBride, and Peter James.*Bury The Bodies* is the fourth book in the series featuring Detective Sergeant Solomon Gray. Buy it now to discover if, in this, the final chapter, Gray will finally find out what happened to his long missing son.

What Others Say

"A stunning book and a series that has become a must read."- **M.W. Craven**, author of the *Washington Poe* series"... deeply emotional, a dark rollercoaster ride."- **Ed James**, author of bestselling *DI Fenchurch* series

What Readers Say

"I follow a lot of Detective series but this is by far one of the best.""You've no idea how glad I am to be back in Gray's world!""The author has such an amazing talent for telling tales.""Hard to put down and gripping to the very end.""There has to be another installment soon!""Wow, this series just gets better.""Another strong instalment in a thoroughly enjoyable series.""A fantastic read with brilliant characters.""A very entertaining and well executed thriller. ""Keith Nixon's latest Solomon Gray murder mystery pushes all the hot button issues of a traumatised post-Brexit UK in this dark tale of loss, revenge and redemption. Flawed and floored by personal tragedy,

DS Solomon Gray is ready to take his place alongside DS Logan McRae, DS Roy Grace and DCI John Luther. Modern jet-black Brit Noir at its best."- **Tim Baker**, CWA shortlisted author of *Fever City* "A compelling murder mystery with a multilayered and engaging new hero. Great read."- **Mason Cross**, author of the *Carter Blake* thriller series "A damaged detective, haunted by a tragic past, a young son missing or dead, a man on a quest for redemption. Detective Sergeant Solomon Gray is a fine creation and Dig Two Graves an intriguing, nourish mystery. Keith Nixon is a sparkling crime fiction talent."- **Howard Linskey**, author of the *Detective Ian Bradshaw* crime series

Also by Keith Nixon

Dark Heart, Heavy Soul

Standalone
The Solomon Gray Series: Books 1 to 4: Gripping Police
Thrillers With A Difference

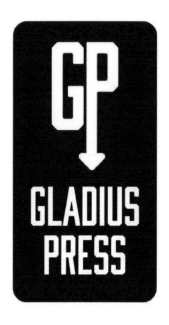

About the Publisher

Gladius Press is a small, yet highly innovative publisher of crime, humour and historical fiction novels based in Manchester in the UK.

Printed in Great Britain
by Amazon